Unscripted
The Hustle
(Book Two)

A Novel By

DONISHA DERICE
and
JAI DARLENE

Scripted Empire

Copyright © 2015 Donisha Derice and Jai Darlene

Library of Congress Catalog-in-Publication Data Available

ISBN
978-0-9971433-9-3 (paperback)
978-0-9971433-3-1 (digital)

Cover design: Kim R. Graham

Scripted Empire

Also by Donisha Derice and Jai Darlene
A Means To An End (The Hustle)

Coming Soon
#WhereIsMave

Prologue

Beau

"Beau! Beau!" A gang of reporters posted up right outside my office building immediately begin to hover over my petite body like vultures when I step out the door. What could they possibly want?

"Now you all know I don't do media. Besides, I don't have any news for you anyway. No new basketball superstar contracts negotiated. No mega endorsement deals signed, sooo..." I sigh at the only downside of being a sports attorney and being married to a professional athlete: the media. I will not let them ruin my lovely afternoon. The sunlight bouncing off the gold building mingles with the flashes of cameras. I smile and throw on my Prada sunglasses. The wind whips through my long tresses as I walk through the crowd of reporters and photogs.

Ugh! I wish I didn't wear these high heels today. My 5-inch black patent leather Gucci pumps click on the concrete sidewalk as I try to get away from these paid-to-be-nosey folks. I am determined to make my stroll to the corner and buy some fresh corn for dinner tonight from the weekly farmer's market.

"How do you feel about your little sister Angel and her bestie Kylie, your brother-in-law's sister, being on *Sports Wives*?" a tall skinny brunette asks, sticking a mic in front of me with a bunch more reporters following behind her.

"I have no idea what you are talking about," I laugh it off. "*Sports Wives*?" I scoff, rolling my eyes at the idea. They wouldn't dare. Angel and Kylie have spent the past few years getting their lives together. Angel finally took her butt to college and is in an accelerated law program, about

1

to graduate soon, and Kylie has her beautiful family with Logan and little Ethan. There's no way they would get involved with some crazy reality TV show.

"So you don't know that they are currently filming a new installment of *Sports Wives* in Atlanta?" Another microphone is shoved inches from my mouth.

"I said what I said," I reply in my best Nene Leaks voice before I push the mic away and continue to walk down the street. Hey, I like to watch the reality TV drama but by no means do I want my family a part of it. We have way too many secrets to be smiling on camera.

"Well...we got the scoop that Skylar Jennings, your husband's ex-girlfriend, is also starring on the show," a voice probes while following behind me as I head down Delaware Street.

"Rumor has it that you stole Israel from Skylar and you two even got into a physical altercation over him," another annoying voice says, trying to get a rise out of me. I quickly stop in my heels and feel several bodies and microphones hit me in the back.

I turn and lift up my glasses.

"Have a great day and enjoy this sun," I say before giving them all a smile and wink like I couldn't care less about the gossip they just spilled. I am going to kill Angel and Kylie. What in the world are they thinking? My cocoa skin tries to mix in with the mostly white crowd as I disappear into the crowd of shoppers at the farmer's market. The gaggle of paparazzi can't keep up. I dig my phone out of my purse to call Bella. I cannot call Angel right this moment. I will go off. Not only is she doing a television show, but with Skylar. There is no way this can end well.

"Hey, B," Bella answers the phone sounding all relaxed and happy.

2

"Where are you?" I fume, biting down on my lip as I exit the farmer's market and head to the parking garage.

"Home. What's up?"

"Did you know about Angel and Kylie doing a reality TV show?"

"What? No way! For real?" I can tell Bella is just as surprised as me. I am usually the last in the family to know of any crazy shenanigans and Bella is usually the first, but this time it looks like she is out of the loop, too.

"Girl, *Sports Wives ATL*, and guess who is also starring on the show?"

"Eww, Cordell Stewart. You know I heard he's dating—"

"What? No. Skylar!" I scream into the phone, cutting Bella off. I am so pissed. Angel knows how private I am about my family, especially to avoid my past coming up.

"Yeah right. No way!" Bella sounds more excited and interested than concerned.

"Reporters were outside my office asking questions about Skylar and me. They brought up the time I beat her up. I mean, what if other stuff comes out? You know we have too much dirt to be dug up and those reality TV shows are unscripted and thrive on drama."

"Look, I am sure Angel knows what she is doing, Beau. She would not go on a television show without having a plan. And please believe Kylie is not going to let anything ruin her perfect little family. They know the script and will stick to it," Bella tries to defend Angel and Kylie's crazy decision to become reality TV stars.

"I am on my way to your house. We need to talk to them. And don't get any ideas. You are not doing a reality TV show."

"I know, I know. Although—"

3

"No, Bella," I laugh before hanging up. I can see those green eyes of hers gleaming with stars in them. She would do awesome on one of those shows, too. She's beautiful, a socialite, philanthropic, and rich. I could go on and on about how Bella would be reality TV gold. There is only one reason why it would never work: the hustle.

Bella

"No, Bella," I mock Beau's words, amused at how upset she is. I don't know why Beau would think I had any remote interest in doing a reality TV show. As fun as it may sound, I've worked hard to get my life on track and I'm not willing to risk it just to be on TV.

"Mama are you talking to yourself?" Aphrodite asks, skipping into the room. My green almond-shaped eyes stare back at me big and bright while Brian's curly golden locks bounce every which way and her perfectly tanned olive skin shines as she gleefully jumps in my lap. With my mother being Italian and Brian's Irish heritage, it's hard to see Aphrodite's African-American roots at just a glance.

God, I have fought so hard to get my family back together and Kylie and Angel know this—especially Kylie, who cried, begged, and pleaded for my forgiveness more than her own, and who reasoned for my pardon from exile better than any attorney I have ever heard. Four years ago, Brian left me, and even after he found out about all the pain I had endured, he still stayed away. He hated me for keeping the truth from him. He despised me because of my past indiscretions and loathed the fact that he still cared about me. But one day he came home. He came back to me and I have Kylie to thank for that.

When Brian finally came home to "work things out" it

4

took him months before he was able to talk to me and look at my growing baby bump, unsure if it was his seed growing inside of me, and doubtful of the DNA test results. In our huge mansion I still felt alone, like we lived on two separate planets. Counseling? Please. It only brought out more ugly secrets from my past. I never gave up, though, and Kylie was always there for me.

"Brian, how can you forgive me so easily and not forgive Bella?" she asked. "How is what she did more egregious than what I have done? Everything she has done, so have I. Mine was for the hell of it. Bella did it as a means to an end to ensure she would never have to live the life she saw destroy her parents." I remember hearing Kylie argue for me. At that point I didn't have a voice. There was nothing I could have said to Brian to make him hear me, but Kylie stood as my champion and it worked.

"Bella, I am ready." Brian's deep blue eyes looked at me wearied and full of concern. The same day Kylie had said those words on my behalf he came to me and told me he was ready to really try and fix us. I thought that I had lost him forever but he pulled me into his arms and I felt his tears rain down on me.

"I see you." He looked into my tired green eyes and I believed him.

"Brian, I am so sorry. I swear…" I tried to apologize. I felt like he needed to know how sorry I was for what I had done to us.

"Shhh," he quieted me.

"No. I'm sorry." I sniffled back tears, prepared to take all the responsibility for our broken marriage.

"Bella, I never allowed you to show me who you really were. Deep down I knew growing up the way you did, there had to be some darkness inside you. I saw the

5

pain behind your beautiful face, but I ignored it. I found myself content with the perfection you put on every day, knowing a rose as beautiful as you must have thorns hidden somewhere."

That night, when Brian said those words, I felt truly reborn, like every awful thing in my past was gone. Brian and I laid together and cried without words until the sun rose and then we got up and started rebuilding our lives.

I won't let anything ruin what I have worked so hard to rebuild. Just like Beau, if my past is dug up it will bury me and everything I love. Kylie and Angel know this and should also know I will do whatever is necessary to protect my family.

"Mommy?" Aphrodite pulls me out of my thoughts.

"Yes, baby?" I smile at her.

"Why did you say *no, Bella?*" Her inquisitive eyes look for an answer.

"Just thinking of something Tia Beau said," I finally answer her.

"Tia Beau said what?" Beau walks in the room on cue.

"Speak of the devil!" Aphrodite giggles.

"What? Did you just call your tia el Diablo?" Beau picks up my mini me. I can tell Aphrodite will have my long legs and modelesque build when she grows up. I brush my curly locks out my face and smile at Beau spinning my baby around and tickling her. I shake my head at why my 4-year-old knows how to use that phrase in proper context. I will blame it on the fact that her favorite auntie is an attorney and Christian who swears she has been in a room with lots of devils.

"No, Tia. Tu es una angelita just like Tia Angel." Aphrodite calls Beau an angel just like Angel, which is normally how their little game goes, but today Beau is not happy with Angel and is definitely thinking she is el Diablo right now.

"Aphrodite, are you ready to go for our walk?" Esmeralda, our maid, asks as she walks into the room. Like clockwork, she is always right on time.

"Awww, but Tia just got here!" Aphrodite pouts as Esmerelda leads her out the door.

"I cannot believe them, Bella. Come on, you have to know how bad this can go," Beau fusses as soon as Esmeralda and Aphrodite leave the room.

"Yes, Beau, we all have a lot at stake if—"

"If any of our past business gets out," Beau finishes my thoughts. I see her brain spinning, probably with all kinds of legal angles and defenses.

"Okay, let's just call and tell them they cannot do this show."

"If they are already filming that means they are tied into a legally binding contract. Plus quitting now will make it look like we all have something to hide."

"So then what do we do?"

"I don't know if there is anything we can do other than pray this doesn't backfire in all of our faces. I am calling Angel. You call Kylie. We need to talk to them now." Beau pulls her phone out of her purse and I grab mine off the table.

"We are all supposed to be leading normal lives. What better way to do that then going on a reality TV show?" I ask sarcastically.

Beau scoffs, punching the screen on her phone super hard. "Stupid, dumb reality TV show. I'll kill them." I laugh at Beau mumbling. I can tell she's furious. Angel and Kylie better know how to hustle for the cameras.

1
Off-Screen Battles

Kylie

Swoosh! Swoosh! The water whistles as it rampages around my head. I feel Logan's grip tighten on my blonde curls and roughly jerk my head up as I desperately gasp for air. My face is dripping wet and my knees are sore as I kneel on the hard marble floor.

"Bitch, what do you mean you're about to get your trust fund? My money is not good enough for you? Look around. Take a good look around. I paid for this home. Everything I've done for you when you had nothing and you think you're going to leave me?" Logan growls. With a fistful of my hair in his hand he turns my head in every direction, forcing me to look around the luxurious bathroom. With the force he uses to turn my head I think my neck is going to snap. The muscles in his biceps glisten as he turns my head, forcing me to look at him. Logan is not fair-skinned but he's not tan either. He looks kind of like Channing Tatum when he starred in G.I. Joe.

"That's not what I meant. I was just saying that—"

"That's your problem," Logan cuts me off. "You are always saying something. Learn to be a submissive wife and shut the fuck up!"

I don't even try to respond; it would be useless. Logan thrusts my head back into the black porcelain throne laden with crystals. The crystals are a little gaudy for my taste, but Logan insisted. He's a self-made millionaire and loves to flaunt it unlike me, who was born into wealth.

I hold my breath, wondering how much longer I can endure his torture. I can't really blame Logan. I do talk too much. I can only blame myself for putting up with his antics for the last two years, but what's done is done. I made the mistake of marrying him and now I'm stuck with him, at least until I get my trust fund, which I'm now wishing I hadn't mentioned to him. Since he was going off on a ridiculous tirade about how he didn't like the dress I have on or the makeup I'm wearing, I thought I would mention to him just how much money I'm set to receive from my trust fund. I was throwing it in his face, almost taunting him, when I told him I will receive the first installment when I turn 25. He took it that I'm already making plans with that money, and I am. Money can't buy a lot of things, but it can buy freedom. I can't deny he has been my financial support, my backbone, and my lover since I met him, but I can only take so much of getting slapped around, cussed out, and disrespected.

I start to feel dizzy. My face has been in the water too long. I know he will pull my head up soon. I know he won't let me drown in a toilet. Every year it gets worse and worse, but he has never hurt me so bad that I needed medical attention. He doesn't want his public persona of the All-American Boy tarnished. Not a moment too soon, Logan yanks my head up. I am panting and fighting to catch my breath.

I can hear my two-year-old crying for his mommy. The door to our bedroom is closed and I can hear him banging his tiny little fists on it.

"Honey, let me go check on Ethan," I beg Logan.

"Where's the fucking nanny? That's what I pay her for!" Logan hisses, clutching a handful of my hair.

"I gave her the rest of the day off."

"So who's supposed to watch him while you film, genius?"

Logan forces my head back under and Ethan's cries drown out. I stop worrying about myself and worry about my child. He must have climbed over the child safety gate in his playroom. I hope he doesn't fall down the stairs. I don't resist Logan. The less I resist the quicker this will be over and the quicker I can get to Ethan.

Logan tugs my hair, yanking my head out of the water. I want to run to Ethan, but Logan hasn't given me permission to get off the floor. I know if I get up he will yank me back to the floor by my hair.

Wheezing, I beg, "Please let me go to Ethan." I feel a nauseous sensation. I feel bile creeping up my esophagus and then I throw up. My head throbs as I watch my breakfast floating in the toilet. "Let me rinse my mouth out."

"Okay." Logan shoves my head back into the porcelain throne. I wasn't expecting that. It happens so quickly I don't have time to hold my breath. I dive face first into my own puke with my mouth open. I can't breathe. I swallow the dirty toilet water as I gasp for air. I begin to throw up again and choke on my own vomit. Choking and gasping, I panic. I swing my arms around looking for anything to hold on to and push myself away from the toilet. My hand falls onto the lever and I flush the toilet. Face still in the toilet, I feel the water quickly swirl downward draining. I only have a few seconds to catch my breath before it re-fills. I hear Logan's curses and Ethan's cries as the water rises, re-submerging my face.

Stupid. Stupid. Stupid. Out of frustration with myself I slap the side of the toilet and cut my finger on the crystals. I feel my warm blood creeping down my arm. That wasn't smart of me to flush the toilet. I know how to deal with Logan. If he thinks I'm fighting back it will only get worse.

11

I've should have never flushed the water. I just made Logan even more upset. I should have just taken it like a woman instead of trying to flush my problems away.

Logan is still holding my head in the toilet. I can feel his rage as he pushes my face deeper into the water. Tears well up in my eyes and before they can drip down my face, toilet water washes them away. I messed up and I'm not sure if I'm going to make it. I can't hold my breath for too much longer. My body goes limp. Logan snatches my head back.

"Breathe, bitch, breathe. You better not die." He halfheartedly tries to kick my stomach. I cross my arms over my belly, protecting myself.

"Please, Logan. Please stop," I beg.

"You still don't know when to shut up. I don't think you learned your lesson."

I take a deep breath of air as he dunks my head in the toilet again. At least I knew it was coming this time. I don't resist and I hold my breath. I silently say a Hail Mary. I have to get through this so I can get to my child. My head is yanked out of the toilet. Logan is tightly gripping my hair, lifting me off my knees into a squatting position. I hear the doorbell ringing and Ethan crying.

Logan leans in close and in a low deep voice says, "I know your secrets and your past. Your trust fund can't save you from me."

I don't respond to his threats. I address the more important issue. "I need to go check on our son."

"The camera crew is here. Get yourself together. I'll get Ethan," Logan snarls as he tosses me like a rag doll and walks off. My back slams against the wall and I fall to the floor. In the distance I hear Logan baby talking to Ethan. His voice is so soft and gentle. Ethan's cries die down.

Breathing heavily, I gasp for air. I look over at my reflection in the floor-to-ceiling mirror; face dripping wet, make up smeared, hair wild, dress ruined. It wasn't worth it. Shutting him down in retaliation to him ranting about how I look wasn't worth the humiliation of almost being drowned in a toilet. He wins. He won this battle, but when I get my trust fund I will win the war.

"Only a few more weeks," I whisper to myself.

2
Eat, Pray, Smile for the Camera

Angel

I grab my chai tea latte off the Keurig and nibble on a bagel as I head up to the study. I am too nervous to really eat, but I force myself to. There is so much going on so quickly. I have gone from being a friend of a wife on *Sports Wives* to being the sixth wife. Well, technically Daniel and I aren't married yet but hell, half of the "wives" on those shows aren't married. Daniel and I have been dating for almost a year and it feels real. I know that he loves me. He has to love me to talk to his father the way he did and force him out of ownership of the Atlanta Eagles.

I'd like to think he did it all for me, but I know it is much deeper than that. His father's comments about me are what sparked the flame, and even though he doesn't know it, I heard every vile, mean, and racist thing Dennis Silver said, and it hurt me to my core. I didn't know ignorance like that still exists. It feels like just yesterday. It's been less than a week and the media just stopped camping out in front of the house yesterday.

His words haunt my thoughts: "Fuck 'em, son. Fuck 'em all you want. I had a black girl once. The best pussy I ever had, so fuck her good, son. But you are supposed to be my heir. How can I pass on my legacy to you when you blatantly disrespect our family?" he said to Daniel with disgust. "You don't parade your pretty black whore around the fucking games posting pictures all on the Instagram and you sure as hell don't fucking marry them. It would be different if she acted like a delicate Latina, Greek, or Italian girl. She could pass as an exotic, but damn it, it is like she

15

is proud of being black," Dennis continued to insult my Colombian and African-American heritage. "Why couldn't you just stay with Savannah? She is perfect; beautiful, smart, and comes from a good family," Dennis said, bringing up Daniel's ex. I am sure he meant to mention the fact that she is white, too.

I stood in Daniel's kitchen holding back tears and curses. I had come over to surprise them with dinner. They had no idea I was there. Daniel is the first white guy I ever dated and I was beginning to regret it. I had seen Mr. Silver at several games and he always seemed cordial, but in that moment I knew how he really felt about me. I quietly placed all the groceries I had bought to make bandeja paisa, a traditional Colombian dish and my favorite meal, into the refrigerator. My heart hurt listening to him spew his disgusting opinions. I wanted to jump out and give him a piece of my mind but instead I just listened.

Daniel had proposed to me the day before his father's tirade and his subsequent announcement of his retirement. Daniel had the Eagles dancers and it seemed like every fan at the game participate in a flash mob dance. Tears streamed down my face when he walked to center court and bent down on one knee. I didn't care what anyone else thought. My heart was so full of joy that I didn't even care about the cold hug I received from Mr. Silver right after the proposal. I figured he was just concerned that his son was getting serious with me too fast.

A day later I had learned the truth; the son of bitch is racist. I stood in that kitchen feeling my emotions about to explode, waiting for Daniel to defend me, but all I heard was Dennis Silver continue to talk about black people. "It's not slavery," he said, making a ridiculous comparison between slavery and the professional basketball league.

"They are not working for free. I pay them real good and that puts food on their tables, clothes on their backs, and roofs over their heads." He gave a condescendingly smug laugh. I still hadn't heard Daniel say a word. I needed him to say something. I can't marry a man that doesn't stand up against racism, regardless of who it comes from. I began to think maybe Daniel knew how his father felt all this time and he was dating me to get under his skin. Or maybe Daniel was hoping that I would act like a 'delicate Latina' or whoever the hell his father thinks would be a more suitable woman for him to date. I felt hot and like I was suffocating. I just wanted to get out of that house. I slowly started tiptoeing to the door, my head spinning from everything I'd heard.

"What the hell is wrong with you?" Daniel's voice overpowered his father's and instantly stopped Dennis' rant.

"Keep your ignorant, racist opinions to yourself! I love her, I am going to marry her, and one day we will have children together and I will love them with all my heart. You will not disrespect Angel," Daniel defended my honor and he didn't stop there.

"I have tolerated so much of your bullshit, Dad, but enough is enough! I am done covering for your ignorance. You will be retiring. I expect your announcement tomorrow. You can either do it gracefully or I will make it happen." Daniel sounded like he was in control. Dennis was silent.

"There is no place in the professional basketball league for you or your ignorant beliefs so you will be removed. There is no place in this family for that shit either, especially with my future wife and future kids. Until you figure out how wrong your beliefs are, I have nothing to say to you, Dad. You need to leave now," Daniel demanded. I quietly left out of the house, smiling from ear to ear, proud of the man that I am going to marry.

Daniel called me right after his father left and I pretended I was right up the road, on my way to see him. I could tell that Daniel was hurt and distraught about something but he wouldn't go into details, trying to spare my feelings. When I saw him he hugged me tight and kept telling me how much he loved me. I remember thanking God for Daniel, like I do every day. It meant even more to me that day at that moment.

Daniel showed even more honor and dignity by allowing his father to gracefully bow out of ownership of the Atlanta Eagles and save face. Daniel could have called his father out, but chose not to and I respect that. And just like that, Daniel went from the Atlanta Eagles president of operations to being the youngest owner of a professional basketball team, thus my promotion on the reality TV show.

Everything that happened with Daniel and his father and the Atlanta Eagles put me in the spotlight. I don't mind the publicity. It has helped me, but my life's goal is not to marry rich or become a reality TV star. After soul searching I figured out what I really want to do; I want to be an actress. Now I just have to tell Bella and Beau. "God, give me the strength to break the news to my sisters, especially to my big sister Beau," I pray. I love my sister, especially her strength and independence. She is part of the reason I decided to go to college. But now I want to inspire people through the characters I play.

I have been taking classes and auditioning for roles for quite some time now. After hustling men out of their money and doing all those music videos, I figure I am already a trained actress. I love getting into character, but hustling and videos only allowed me to play pretty and sexy. I want to push myself, which is why I enrolled into acting classes. A crack head, a single mother, a doctor...I find myself pushing it to the limits and I am good at it. Now I just have to figure out how to tell my sisters I dropped out of school less than a year before I am supposed to graduate so that I can pursue acting full time.

I sit at my desk waiting for GG to call for our morning prayer and Bible study. GG knows I haven't been to church since moving to Atlanta about two years ago, so she makes sure I am keeping God in my life. I really don't have any excuse for not going to church, so I really do appreciate the mornings with GG, all six of them. She gives me Saturday off. I pick up my Bible and turn to Proverbs 15:22. *Without counsel purposes are disappointed: but in the multitude of counselors they are established.* I did discuss my career change with GG and prayed about it for months before I left school. I feel confident about my choice and I honestly do see God opening doors for me.

Now I need God and GG's counsel on how to deal with the situation with Daniel and his family. I am not built to be fake or put up with people's bull so if I am going to marry Daniel, Lord help me.

"Morning, GG. How are you doing?" I answer GG's call with a smile.

"GG is blessed and highly favored, as always. I am so glad to hear ya' bright smiling voice. Father God, I just want to thank you for another beautiful day," GG begins prayer. "Lord, I ask for you to continue to watch over Angel Maria Jimenez-Jones. Continue to bless her, Father God, as she continues her walk with you and begins new journeys in her life."

I giggle a little bit at GG's prayer, but wait until after the prayer is done before commenting. "Man GG, my whole name? God and I still aren't on a first name basis yet?" I crack jokes and hear GG is laughing too.

"Girl, hush yo' mouth. Did you choose a scripture?" GG gets back to business.

"Yes, ma'am." I pick my Bible up and go back to the Proverb I had read right before she called. "GG, I think it is time for me to talk to Beau and Bella." I sigh deeply. Yes, I am a grown woman but I still dread having certain conversations with my big sisters, who act more like my mothers. Waiting for some wise words from GG, I hear my doorbell.

"Shit," I mumble." The producers from *Sports Wives* are over an hour early. They said 8 o'clock. I grab my strapless LBD off the bed and slide into it."

"Girl, is you cussing while I'm trying to help save yo' soul?" I hear GG fussing through the phone.

"No, GG. I am so sorry. I have an appointment and they are super early. Can we finish later? I love you." I hang up before she can respond. I slip on a pair of Manolo Blahnik ankle strap sandals and fluff my curly hair in the mirror while checking myself out. I dab my full lips with lipstick until they turn rose pink and splash on my Daisy by Marc Jacobs perfume. I snap my watch onto my left wrist and slide a few diamond bangles on my right. I stop and glance in the mirror in the foyer and do a quick twirl to make sure I look good, peeking over my shoulder at my perfectly round butt.

"Good morning," I say as I open the door with a smile that instantly turns into a jaw-dropping look of confusion.

"Que, linda! You look so beautiful, mija. Don't just stand there; give your mama a hug!" My mother, who I haven't seen face to face in over ten years, grabs me in her arms. I don't hug her back. Still in shock, I stand there frozen and speechless.

What is she doing here? My eyes start darting every which way, looking for her husband—the man that made her choose between him or me. "Where is Alejandro? Why are you here?" I break from her hug and pull her into the house. Staring at her, she is as beautiful as I remember with her perfectly tanned skin and long curly hair just like mine. I look down at her, waiting for her to give me answers and trying to figure out how to get her out of my house before the producers and cameras show up.

"Alejandro did not come with me. I came to see my beautiful daughter. I have missed you so much, Angel." Her hand rubs my cheek. I don't believe anything she is saying.

"You have to go." I grab her arm and look down at my watch. It's ten minutes after seven. Yeah, some may think this is a cold way to treat my mother, but she hasn't been a mother to me in almost fifteen years. Birthday and Christmas presents and three calls a year doesn't make her a mother, at least not to me.

"Is that any way to treat your mother, Angel Maria Jimenez?" She pulls away from me, slipping out of her two-inch black heels. I notice she is wearing a stewardess uniform. "This is such a beautiful home, mija." She starts walking through the house glancing into the great room and then the dining room. She stops at the kitchen. "You have done very well for yourself, Angel. I always knew that you would." She grabs my left hand, focusing on the 12 carats on my ring finger.

"Did you not hear me, Maria? You have to go," I restate firmly as I force myself out of her grasp. How dare she just pop up out of nowhere and expect me to be happy to see her? I don't resent her for what she did because I know my life would have turned out so differently. I would have never met my family or Daniel. But I know she made the decision out of selfishness because she didn't want to lose her rich drug dealer husband.

"I can't," she says as her eyes get watery.

"What do you mean you can't? I haven't seen you in so long. Why are you here?'

"I can't go back to him." Tears start running down her face. Her dimpled smile has disappeared, revealing fear and worry.

"What?" I stare her in her eyes and she seems broken. I can't put her out. No matter what she did, she gave me life and I know how I am treating her is not what God expects of me.

"Angel, I know you think that I just tossed you to the side and chose Alejandro over you, but that is not it at all. If you would have stayed your life would have been as miserable as mine has been for the past fifteen years. I let you go to save you. You have to believe that, mija." She pulls me into her arms and I don't pull away this time.

I hold on to her for a few minutes crying with her. I have always wanted answers from her and this may be the only chance I get.

"I understand if you want me to leave, Angel, but I do need you to know that I love you and have always loved you. What I did was because I loved you." My mother steps back and looks into my eyes.

Looking deep into her eyes, she seems so tired and weary, like she hasn't slept or rested in days. "I'll run you a bath," I say as I take her hand and lead her up to a bathroom and turn on the bath. I don't completely understand why this is happening right now but I will take care of her.

I walk out of the bathroom and hold back tears. God,

that could have been me. If I had grown up in Colombia around the drugs and that lifestyle, I would be broken just like her. She saved my life and I now I have to save hers.

"Mamá?" I open the bathroom door to give her towels.

"Angel, get out!" she screams at me. I just stare at her squatting over the toilet. She has packs of heroin spread across a hand towel on the floor as she digs more out of the toilet. I hear plops as more packs fall out of her ass into the toilet.

"Oh my God! Oh my God!" I scream, closing the door. "How could you bring this into my home? Into my life?" I talk to her from the other side of the door.

"Mira, mira." The bathroom door flies open and she commands me to look in. "Angel, I am 47 years old. Do you honestly think I would choose to do this? Every last one of those packs I had to swallow and fly for over three hours with them in my stomach. Then I had to shit them out in the toilet, dig them out of my own shit, and clean them. This is what he forces me to do now. He says I am old and no longer beautiful. He says he is disgusted by me and allows other putas to lie in my bed. I cannot do this anymore, Angel. I cannot go back to this life. And believe me, had you stayed in Colombia this too would have been your life. Mira." She grabs my face into her hands, forcing me to look at her.

I look at her and I see myself deep in her eyes. "I will take care of you," I promise. "Mamá , I am going to fix this for you. But right now I have to go to work. I am going to fix you some changua for breakfast and leave it in the guest room right across the hall. Please get some rest and we will talk as soon as I get home, but Mamá, you have to promise me that you will stay in the house and lay low." The doorbell rings as I am holding her in my arms.

"Claro, Angel. Te lo prometo," she promises. I step into the guest bathroom and wrap all the packs up into a towel. I walk into my closet and place the drugs into a shoebox. The doorbell rings again and then my phone starts ringing. I wash my hands and face and quickly touch up my makeup. I look into my mirror and check myself out before heading downstairs. I take a deep breath, open the door, and smile for the camera.

Donisha Derice & Jai Darlene

3
Show Time

Kylie

I can hear the camera crew downstairs setting up. I crawl over to the bathroom door to lock it, too devoid of energy to get off the floor and walk. The crew is not allowed in my bedroom, but you never know. I would hate for someone to accidently stumble into my bathroom and see me dripping in piss water and puke. My stomach feels queasy just thinking about it. I hurl into the toilet again.

I wipe my face with the back of my hand and sink back onto the floor. I need to quickly get myself together, but I sit on the floor a little while longer. I'm just not up to facing the world right now. I want to sit here on this floor and cry until the tears can't come anymore. Too bad I don't have that luxury. Too bad it's show time and I have to put on a mask and pretend like everything is peachy.

I slowly begin to get up off of the floor, taking my time. I hear my phone vibrating on the counter. I look at caller ID and see that it's GG. My first instinct is to ignore her, but I decide against it. I don't feel like talking, but GG always has a way of calling when I need her.

"GG," I say, trying to disguise the tremble in my voice from crying.

"Hey, baby. What's the matter?" GG asks, sounding alarmed.

"Nothing." I stare at my horrible reflection in the mirror. My hair is wet and tangled. Snot is dripping from my nose. My eyes are bloodshot and my face is flushed.

"I know something's wrong. I can hear it in your voice. It's that show, isn't it?" GG guesses. "Angel told me all about that reality stuff y'all doing. It must be hard."

"That and I just feel like I've made horrible decisions in my life that I may never recover from." Even if I can't reveal everything, I feel a little better confiding in GG.

"You can't beat yourself up over your past mistakes, baby. People tend to want to pick and choose their sins, but technically in the eyes of the Lord all sin is equal and we all have sinned. A thief is no better than a murderer. And if they both repent, God will give both the thief and the murderer the same forgiveness and wipe both their sins away. So what that means for you, my sweet child, is that there is nothing that you can't recover from. There's nothing that you can do that God won't forgive you for. You just have to learn how to forgive yourself and make your situation work for you. Make the best out of a bad situation. Like that one hoe with the sex tape."

"GG!" I gasp and we both giggle.

"You know what hoe I'm talking about." I hear GG snap her fingers as she tries to recall. "She laid it low and spread 'em wide. She was put to shame and she probably thought life couldn't get any worse. And you know what she did? She built an empire from it. You doing this show ain't as bad as doing a sex tape, so surely you can turn your situation around for the better."

"You're right, as always," I say, still giggling.

"Now come on, let's pray. I know you're catholic but it's the same God." I close my eyes and listen to the power of GG's words. "Dear heavenly Father, we come together today to thank you for giving us another day of life. Another day to turn our situation around for the better. Amen."

"What? That's it?"

"Yeah, that's all you need, honey."

"Thank you, GG. I have to go."

"I know. That's why I kept it short for you. Talk to you later, sweetie." I hang up the phone feeling a lot better than I did before I answered it.

The doorknob rattles and someone rapidly knocks, making me jump. I almost slip and fall.

"Open the door," Logan demands. I immediately unlock and open the door for fear that if I don't move quickly enough he will kick it down and make my day way worse than it already is. "Why is this door locked?"

"I didn't want anyone to accidently see me not looking my best, honey," I meekly answer, playing the submissive role like I learned my lesson today.

Logan looks me up and down in disgust. "Hurry up. Your outfit is laid out on the bed."

I nod my head and feel relieved as he walks out of the room. I don't want any more battles, not today, so I do what he asks. I quickly shower, put a Band-Aid on my finger, brush my teeth, and blow-dry my hair. I walk into the bedroom and find my outfit lying across the bed: a nude bra, a button-up black peep-through lace shirt with a white collar and cuffs, a pair of white slim fit trousers, and a pair of black gladiator wedge sandals with giant gold studs. It is elegant and risqué all at the same time and it will look astonishing on my tall and slender frame. I have to admit, the man can put an outfit together but it's still not what I wanted to wear. I wanted to wear my dress before he ruined it.

Logan barges back in, closing the door behind him. He ignores my naked body and directs his attention to my outfit smiling.

"So what do you think?" he asks, gesturing to the outfit.

"I like it. I really do." I hesitate, trying to figure out the best way to word what I'm about to say next without setting him off again. "But um, I just don't understand why you didn't like what I had on before."

"Because it made you look like a slut. White trash," he tells me, never taking his eyes off the outfit.

I gesture to the blouse. "But the top you picked out is see-through and I'll have on nothing but a bra underneath."

"There's a difference between being suggestive and being a slut. God, you are stupid." He runs his fingers through his hair. "The last public image the world has of you is a wild, trashy, drugged out party girl. This right here will elevate your persona from Lindsey Lohan to Elizabeth Taylor." He finally turns to me and looks me in my eyes. "I'm upgrading you."

Logan gently strokes my cheek and kisses my forehead. I don't know how he 180s so quickly from pushing my face into a toilet to kissing it.

"Okay. I'll wear it with pride. I will embody everything Elizabeth Taylor stands for." I smile, fighting the uncontrollable urge to roll my eyes instead.

"Good. Then you can stop questioning my decisions as the man of this household and get dressed." He harshly twists my nipple. He has twisted my nipple so much I'm numb to it. I don't even flinch.

Logan leaves me to my peace and quiet and I quickly get dressed and hurry down the stairs. Ethan is on the sofa bouncing on the lap of his Aunty Angel as she chats with Logan. Angel Eskimo kisses Ethan and I smile. I notice our nanny out of the corner of my eye standing in the corner gripping my son's stroller. Logan must have made her come back to work after I gave her the day off.

"Angel, you effing diva you." I approach Angel and

lean down to give her a hug.

"Wow. Look at you. Girl, you are snatched." Angel snaps her fingers, referring to how good I look in my outfit. She eyes my cut finger. "Even your Band-Aid is blinged out. What happened?" she asks as she lifts my hand to get a better look at the bejeweled all black Band-Aid.

"I cut it slicing up fruit for Ethan," I lie, unfazed.

Logan picks up Ethan from Angel's lap. "I'm going to take my boy to the park and work on his throwing arm," Logan says, beaming with pride as he walks out the door with the curvaceous nanny trailing behind him. He hates to have her off the clock. I'm 80% sure that they are screwing around. I wonder if he beats her, too. Or maybe he actually loves her in a way he'll never love me. I want to believe he loved me at one point. I think he loved the prestige that came with marrying an heir of the Ethan Rose Pharmaceutical empire, but that love is fading now that he fears it will slip away.

"Awww. Daddy and son time. He is such a great father," Angel notes.

"Yeah, he is such a great father." *And such a horrible husband,* I think to myself.

Angel takes a moment to analyze my face and I do the same to her.

"What's wrong?" We both ask at the same time.

Angel is pursuing acting and for the last two years I have been acting as well, putting on a front like I have the perfect marriage when I don't. So I know what just went down with my husband moments ago is not written on my face. My mask is on. I'm putting on a happy face and Angel seems to be doing the same right now. I can't put my finger on it but something is wrong with her and I can tell she knows something is wrong with me. You don't get to be best friends for over a decade and not be able to emphatically pick up on each other's feelings. That is why I always avoid Angel like the plague after one of Logan's bouts of rage. I'll never tell anyone what he does to me when we're alone.

Before either of us can respond, Shannon, one of the producers of the show, approaches us.

"Ladies, ladies. That was great, but I need to get another shot from a different angle. And then I need you all to elaborate on what's bothering you. Make sure it's spicy." She turns to one of the cameramen. "Did you get the part about the great dad?" she asks him. The cameraman nods.

"Whoa. Wait. You were filming all that?" I ask, almost appalled. She could have at least warned us first. I didn't know this was what I was signing up for when I agreed to be on the show, or, more accurately, forced to be on the show by Logan to magnify his good guy image.

"The cameras are always rolling," she reminds me. "Remember that." I'm tired of not having control of my own life.

My cell phone rings. I look at the caller ID and do not answer it, knowing my older brother will be on the other end of the call. He may have found out about me doing the show and the last thing I need to hear is how I'm being such a big disappointment to the family again.

No sooner after I hit the ignore button on my cell, my cordless land line rings. This time, I do want to answer. The caller ID says RESTRICTED but I know who it is. I've been waiting for this call for a while now and I'm pissed I'm not alone to answer. I bite my lower lip, put my phone on silent, and place it on the coffee table.

"Is that something you need to get? Wait, was that your brother or sister-in-law calling you? I would love to get a shot of you on the phone with them. Are you all getting along? Any family drama? Weren't they supposed to get a divorce?" Shannon's mouth is running a mile a minute.

There is no way I'm bringing my family into this. "No, that wasn't my brother or my sister. Can we just shoot the scene?"

"Action!" Shannon shouts and on cue, Angel lights up for the camera.

"What's wrong?" Angel asks with concern in her eyes. I can't tell if she's acting for the cameras or if she really expects me to spill my guts.

"Cut! Kylie, you were supposed to say 'what's wrong' too, just like the first time. Do it again. Action."

"What's wrong?" Angel and I both ask simultaneously. I want to turn to look at Shannon for a signal that we got it right, but since she didn't interrupt us, I guess we did.

"You first," we both giggle.

"No! You first," Angel insists. I read between the lines. Angel is really not trying to discuss her problems on national TV and we will have to chat about it later off camera.

"Okay, okay. Me first." I smile for the camera. Trying to buy time to think of something spicy to say, I take a sip of the wine that was set out on the table by the producers. Angel has a straight face, but the glare in her eyes says, *What the fuck are you doing? You are a recovering drug addict and alcoholic.* But hell, it's just one glass. I take another sip.

She takes the wine glass from my hand. "Girl, what type of wine is this?" Angel inquires, looking at the glass with curiosity before she sets it on the table. "I know you have nothing but the best."

"It's Grande Cru, shipped from France. My absolute fav'. I like to have a glass from time to time when Logan and Ethan are having daddy-son time."

"So tell me what happened? What's wrong?" Angel asks while accidently, but really on purpose, knocking my two thousand dollar bottle of wine and glass over, spilling it all over my white sheep rug. "Oops," she says.

"Cut! Can we get someone one to clean that up?" Shannon sounds annoyed. A cleanup crew immediately sweeps in.

"Unless you are throwing the wine in someone's face be more careful," Shannon barks at Angel. "Just move the rug out of the way. We don't have time to clean wine stains, and make sure you keep all the shots from their waists up so viewers won't notice the missing rug."

The crew removes the rug and as they set the table back down where it was I notice RESTRICTED light up across the cordless phone again and I come up with an idea.

"Action!" Shannon announces.

"We're best friends, right?" I ask Angel.

"No, we're sisters," Angel quickly counters.

"And I can tell you anything?"

"Claro."

"Speak English. You know the only Spanish word I know is no," I joke.

"Of course," Angel laughs. "Spill the tea already."

I sigh. "Well, I'm honest enough with myself to admit to my sister that my love life is not where it should be."

Angel gasps. She doesn't believe a word I'm saying, but she's playing for the camera.

"Yeah, I mean we still get it *in*, but not as often as we used to before we got married. After the baby I feel like…I don't have it anymore. You know what I mean?"

"I know how to put the spice back in your life! Come on, girl." Angel grabs my hand and takes me upstairs to my room. The cameras are right behind us. "Let's pick out the sexiest outfit we can find."

"I don't think I have anything sexy," I giggle.

"Do you have a cute bra and panty set?" she asks while turning to the camera.

"I guess I do."

"Well go put it on and show 'em the definition of a MILF."

"Angel," I say, shocked and a little embarrassed.

I go into my walk-in closet and find a cute pink and white lacy bra and panty set. I walk out the closet holding up the bra. "Angel, like this?"

"Exactly like that," Shannon says. "Now put it on. We have some interns running out to get candles to set the mood."

"Whoa. Call your interns and tell them you were just playing. I'm not prancing around on camera in my panties, Shannon."

"I'm not saying you have to do it, but it will be tastefully done. If you want to be featured as the star of the show you will do what you have to do to be that star." I get what Shannon is saying. Do it or be reduced to a friend of the show or even fired.

I huff and go back into the closet and slam the door. I text Logan and ask him what to do. I'm damned if I do and damned if I don't. If I do it Logan will probably get upset with me for looking too slutty on TV and if I don't do it and I lose my spot on the show he will get mad at me for losing my spot.

Logan replies, **DO IT!**

A few minutes later Angel walks in and sees my face.

"Are you okay?"

I shake my head no, trying to fight back the tears. I don't want to be half naked on camera. My family will be so disappointed. More importantly, I don't want my son to grow up and one day and Google half naked pictures of me.

"They said there'd be no cameras in the bedroom!" I shout loud enough, hoping Shannon will hear me.

"That's my fault. My bad. I should have never dragged you up here with my bright idea. I had no idea that she would want you to actually put on the lingerie. I'm sorry, Ky." Angel says hugging me. "You know what? Forget Shannon. You don't have to do anything you don't want to do and I'll tell her myself. If you're out I'm out."

"No. No, I'm going to do it. I'll show 'em the definition of MILF like you said." I give a weak smile.

We hear a knock on the door and Angel answers it with the door partially open so whoever it is can't see me crying on the floor. "Angel, we need you for this next scene. Shannon wants to shoot a scene where you are setting up the candles then tiptoeing out the bedroom," a voice says, probably an intern. Shannon, that bitch, just assumes I'm going to prance around on national TV half naked because she says so.

"Damn, you guys went to the store and bought candles just that quick?" Angel asks.

"We got the candles from the production van outside. We keep props on hand just in case."

"Are you sure you want to do this?" Angel turns to me and asks. I nod my head yes and motion for her to go. I put on the bra and panty set and walk out of the closet. Candles are lit around the room. I feel nauseous at all the cameras and people in my bedroom with their eyes glued to my body. My body trembles from the cool temperature in the room. Normally when I make a spectacle of myself I have the decency to be drunk so I won't remember it.

Shannon directs me to the bed covered in roses and there is a bright spotlight on the bed. There is nothing sexy about this at all. I feel awkward with everyone's gawking eyes on me as I nervously walk over to the bed.

"Loosen up, look natural," Shannon directs.

I take one of the flowers and put it in my hair. I think about all the great sex I will be having later and strike a sexy pose. On cue, in walks Logan. His face looks aroused and so does his package.

"You look like a Playboy Bunny. I can't wait to get my hands on you," he says. The camera glides out of the bedroom on a track slider.

"And cut!" I hear Shannon yell.

4
Hustle Behind the Scenes

Angel

Driving home I can't shake the feeling that something is wrong with Kylie. I don't think either of us ever thought about how much of our privacy we would lose doing this show. I know why I am doing it; to get more exposure to help boost my acting career. But I am still not sure why Kylie is doing this. It sucks that we couldn't really talk about what is going on with us. I have to figure out what I am going to do about my mother, and more importantly, what I am going to do with 50 packs of heroin.

I hear my phone singing in my purse. Shoot, I forgot to call Daniel and let him know my mother is at the house. Even worse, the producers are going to be there to film a scene with us. I cannot have my mom wandering in and ending up on television, especially since I don't know what Alejandro is going to try to do to her. She has to stay under the radar.

I check my phone. I have a missed called from a blocked number and no voicemail message. Oh well, must not have been important. I dial Daniel's number. I hope it's not too late to give him a heads up about my mom and make sure she is in her room before the cameras show up.

The private caller calls back before I can finish calling Daniel. "Who is this?" I answer, not trying to mask my irritation with the blocked caller.

"Hola, Angel. Como estas?" Alejandro's voice sounds cold and scary. I was hoping I would be able to avoid ever speaking to him again. I haven't spoken to him since I left Colombia but his powerful voice sounds just the same.

"Hola, Alejandro. Estoy muy bien, y tu?" I try to stay calm. I know a man like him can sense any type of fear or deceit. "It has been so long. Why the call out the blue?" I question him.

"Donde esta tu mama, Angel? Estoy buscando Maria," he gets to the point and asks about my mother.

"I haven't seen my mother since I last saw you, and you know she only calls for birthdays and Christmas. Why would you think I know where she is? Wasn't the point of sending me to the States was to keep us apart?"

"She has something of mine and I want it back," Alejandro ignores my questions and begins making demands.

"Maria no esta aqui," I lie and hope he buys it.

"Bien, bien. If she contacts you call me. Angelita, I need to speak with your mother immediately." I can hear the seriousness in his voice.

"Claro. Tenga un buen dia," I let Alejandro know I understand and tell him to have a good day before hanging up. I let out a deep breath. I think he believed me. I wipe my sweaty palms on my legs. I can feel my hair stick to the back of my neck.

Alejandro is the epitome of the drug lords you see in movies and the real-life legends you've heard of. Think Scarface, Pablo Escobar, and the Corleone family. He is a ruthless man that would kill his own mother to succeed, so there's no doubt he would kill mine if he felt like she was in his way. At least that is what my mother raised me to believe. Even as a little girl I was taught to tread lightly around him, and when he showed me love I was still scared of him. It seems like all my mother attracted on those flights was drug dealers; first my father, then Alejandro. Why couldn't she have met a nice businessman or dated a pilot?

I throw on a smile as I pull up to the house. I never got a chance to warn Daniel about my mom and the camera crew is already here. She picked a hell of a time to pop up at my house with her drug lord husband's dope. For so long I had to lead a double life, but I have done my best to change all of that. Now it seems like I will have to hustle my way out of some more shit all while smiling for the cameras.

"Hey, babe." Daniel leans down to give me a kiss when I get in the house. I wrap my arms around him and hold him tight, not wanting to let him go. He is everything I could hope for in a man: tall and lean with golden hazel eyes and dark curly hair. He is smart, too, with a MBA from Emory. Most importantly, he is honest, never holds punches for anyone, and is a genuinely good man.

"You forgot to tell me we had company," Daniel whispers in my ear as he kisses it. I quickly change the subject.

"Are you excited about the Atlanta Eagles' Night Under the Stars? It's your first event since becoming owner of the team," I gush as Daniel and I walk into the living room and I sit on his lap.

"Yeah, but I'm nervous too. This is a lot of responsibility and I just want to raise money for the Soaring Eagles Charity. It's a charity that raises money for the youth of Atlanta. My dad has raised over $21 million over the past ten years."

"You are going to be great. You have grown up being prepared for this. Plus, you have me. I have raised millions of dollars for my sister's charity, Sophia Tanya Love Thy Children," I give Bella's charity a little plug. "I am going to go get dressed. Baby, don't worry. Everything is going to

40

go wonderfully." I kiss Daniel and stand up. It takes my hair stylist at least two and a half hours to straighten my hair, so I need to start getting ready now.

"I need to get dressed, too, so I can arrive there early," Daniel says, standing up behind me and gently rubbing my butt. I grab his hand and head towards the stairs.

"That was great guys," Evan, one of the producers motions for the cameramen to stop filming. "Angel, can I have a word with you?" he asks, looking concerned. I remember Shannon telling us to keep up the excitement, so I assume that is what Evan wants to talk about, too.

"What's up?" I stop on the stairs, letting Daniel's hand go. I still need a moment alone with Daniel to talk about my mom staying with us, so I hope Evan makes this quick.

"Look, this is a first for me and maybe for reality TV," Evan whispers once Daniel is out of sight. Evan's normally peach face is unusually red, like he is nervous. "When we got here, one of the camera guys caught a glimpse of a petite woman with long curly hair running up the stairs," Evan explains. I start laughing and his face goes from looking concerned to confused. "We thought maybe it was you running up the stairs, because you didn't want to get caught on camera without your makeup on. But then you walked through the door about five minutes later. I sent another camera guy around to the back of the house to see if she was going to sneak out, but she hasn't." Evan starts to stutter a little. "I-I-I think she is still upstairs. How do you want to proceed?" Evan's eyes get big like he is hoping I'll tell him to have the camera guys follow me up there to confront Daniel and whatever whore he has in our house.

I am still laughing and I know Evan has no idea what to expect of me.

"I know who she is and please believe she is not a

41

mistress. Does it look like Daniel would have any desire to cheat?" I twirl around on the steps, showing off my curvy figure.

"No way. You are gorgeous, Angel. It just seemed—"

"It just seems like she doesn't want to be on camera and that's why she ran up the stairs when you arrived. Sorry, Evan, no drama today," I put Evan in check before heading upstairs. I can't help but to notice a slight smirk and look of disbelief on Evan's face as he walks away.

"Mamá ..." I open her bedroom door without knocking. When will I learn? She is sitting on the bed, legs crossed, counting a pile of money, no doubt Alejandro's.

"Please put that away," I whisper, closing the door behind me. "Mamá, Alejandro called me today." I sit on the edge of the bed and she instantly stops fiddling with the money and looks at me as if I had just told her the devil was on his way.

"Mija, what did you tell him? Please tell me you didn't tell him where I am." She frantically starts stuffing the money into a small plastic sack. She is shaking so much that several of the bills fall from her hand before making it into the bag.

"I told him that I hadn't seen you in 15 years and didn't understand why he'd think you would come to me. I think he believed me." I smile nervously.

"Good, good. Angel, I am so sorry I even came here and got you involved in my chaos. I will leave tonight." Mamá stands up and slides into the teal green sandals that match the teal, yellow, and black maxi dress she is wearing.

"No. I am going to figure this out. Just promise me you will stay put. The camera guy and producer saw you today. If Alejandro finds out you are here it is going to be bad for the both of us. I have to go, but I promise it will be okay." I smile again and stand up. "Te amo," I say and rub my fingers through her curly locks. My mother looks very good to be 47 and I can see why Evan would think she was Daniel's sidepiece.

"The producers thought my mom was your mistress," I laugh as I walk into our bedroom. Daniel is fully dressed, looking sexy.

"I thought you and your mom weren't close." Daniel walks over so I can fix his tie.

"We aren't. She just popped up out the blue this morning."

"She seems nice. Is she coming to the gala tonight?"

"She is tired. She flew in from Colombia. I think she just wants to rest."

"Cool. Maybe we can do lunch tomorrow." Daniel kisses my forehead. I don't answer him. I don't want to lie to Daniel but I can't tell him the truth, either.

"I love you," I let Daniel know before he walks out the room. I hear the doorbell ring. It must be my glam squad. In a panic, I hurry into the closet to check the shoe box. The packs are still there. Where else would they be? I shake my head. Daniel wouldn't go through my things. I shove the box into the back of my closet.

I hurry into the bathroom to take a quick shower. If only washing away the dirt in my life was as easy as cleaning off the physical filth. I hear my glam squad setting up to get me dolled up for the gala. Shit, even if covering my dirt was as easy as covering blemishes with makeup, that would be nice. Mamá , heroin, Alejandro I am about to embark on the biggest hustle of my life and probably the most important acting job of my life; smiling for the camera while hustling behind the scenes.

5
Meet The Cast

Kylie

"Everyone out of my house!" Logan demands.

"But Kylie's glam squad is on their way to get her ready for tonight," Shannon reasons.

"She can get herself ready. I come home with the mood set up just right, candles lit, and my wife in pink and white lace. I want some private time, if you know what I mean." Logan slyly grins and he makes me nervous. I want to beg Shannon to take me with her, because when she leaves it's not going to be all sunshine and Hello Kitties.

"I get it. I get it." Shannon smiles. *No, Shannon. Don't do it. Don't go.* She takes her interns, crew, and cameras and leaves. Damn.

Logan is blocking the bedroom door glaring at me. I tremble with dread. He looks ballistic. I'm not going to wait around for him to flip out on me. I run. I race to the closet. If I can get to the closet and lock the door maybe he'll calm down. I hear Logan right behind me. He grabs me by the arm and slams me against the wall. He mushes my face against the wall and yanks my arm behind my back until I feel like it is going to be ripped from my socket. Trying to outrun the top quarterback in the league? What was I thinking?

"Logan, I'm sorry." He told me to put on the lingerie. I checked with him first. So, I don't even know what he's mad about, but I apologize anyway.

"You're sorry? You're sorry? Do you know how you just ruined my repetition? Do you?" he screams in my ear and spittle flies on the side of my face.

"You have got to be the biggest blonde airhead in all of Atlanta. When that scene airs everyone in America is going to think I am an inept pansy that can't keep it up," Logan growls at me.

"I'm sorry. Shannon said—" I was going to explain, or more like tell a small fib about, how it was all Shannon's idea and that she made me say those things, but he cuts me off.

"I don't give a fuck what Shannon said. And I don't give a fuck about you being sorry. If you want to apologize get down on your knees and beg for forgiveness." He grabs me by my hair and forces me to my knees.

"Beg!" He slaps me. Not hard enough to leave a mark, but it still hurts.

I clasp my hands together and beg. "Please, please forgive me. I'm so sorry. You are all man and you satisfy my every need. When I shoot my testimonial I will talk about all the orgasms you give me on a regular basis and that it's my fault that our love life is lacking. Please, babe. I have to get ready for the gala," I reason, trying to change the subject.

"I should make you suck my dick." Logan pushes me away from him. "I'm going to take a shower. Wear that navy blue dress," he commands. "We wouldn't want the same wardrobe disputes that we had this morning." Logan walks away, leaving me to dwell on his threat.

After I put on the stupid blue dress and fab myself up, Logan's mother calls my cell.

"Hello. Where's Ethan? He should be here by now," Logan's mother says in a snippy tone with her strong Southern accent. At least she said hello first before getting straight to the point, which is rare for her.

"Nancy, I know. I know. Logan didn't want to burden

you so our nanny will be caring for him tonight."

"If you knew you wanted to use your nanny then what you call me for?" Before I can explain, she begins an angry rant. "Next time don't call me to watch him! You're just trying to keep me away from my grandson. Your one of *those* mothers, aren't you?"

This lady is crazy and the apple doesn't fall far from the tree. I can't believe in the same breath she told me not to ask her to watch Ethan anymore and said that I'm trying to keep her away from him. Furthermore, I didn't ask her to watch Ethan; she asked me!

I do feel sort a bad for not calling to give her a heads up, but at the end of the day Logan made that decision when he was out there trying to have booty calls with the nanny, and I'm not going to apologize for his actions. I've already been forced to apologize once today and I'm not doing it again. Not today.

"Look, your son wanted the nanny here tonight," I tell her matter-of-factly, "So, you'll have to take your issues up with him. Maybe you can swing by tonight and help the nanny put him to bed."

I can imagine Nancy's face frowning up in anger. "You want me to help the help?! You're crazy! You are so bi-polar."

"What?" I can't believe she's saying that to me when she's the real bipolar cray-cray!

"Yeah, you are. One minute you're all like, *yeah, Ethan needs to be around his grandmother. He loves spending time with you*," she says, mimicking my voice before reverting back to her normal tone. "And the next you're telling me not to come around. My son could have done better." Nancy slams her phone in my ear.

No, I've could've done better. You better believe that

47

marrying into this family is my biggest regret. When I found out I was pregnant, Logan convinced me that marriage was my best option. He pointed out that I didn't want any more scandals involving the Rose name across headlines and that it was the first step to cleaning up my public image. I agreed because I'd put my parents through so much and I just wanted to get my act together and prove to them I can do better despite the fact I chose a different path than what they wanted for me. It was a win-win: marry the one I loved and create a new public persona.

I pray for my own peace of mind. "God, help me out this situation and soon. In the name of the Father, the Son, and of the Holy Spirit, Amen."

"Did you call me?" Logan asks, coming out of the bathroom. He is looking at me so I don't roll my eyes even though I want to. He wishes he was my God.

"Honey, you look amazing. You will stop the show when you walk into the room tonight," he compliments as he kisses me on my cheek.

I have to admit I enjoy these moments when he acts like a normal human being, like how he used to act before we got married. Even after we got married, when I was pregnant, he was so thoughtful, sweet, and charming, but it seemed like the moment I gave birth he literally flipped the script on me. Whenever I disagree with him or go against his wishes, he turns into the Incredible Hulk. As long as I'm doing what he wants and don't talk back to him, we're good, but I never could be controlled. Sometimes I speak my mind and sometimes I don't; it just depends on how I feel that day. Which means sometimes he beats me and sometimes he doesn't. My entire life I have said and done what I want and I'm not going to stop now.

You see, Logan has me in a conundrum. When I was in

love with him, I made the mistake of confiding in him about my secret. When I was young and dumb, at least dumber than what I am now, Angel and I used to hustle. For about four or five years we would meet rich guys at parties, slip them a date rape drug, and then rob them. I didn't need the money. I needed the adrenaline rush hustling gave me. We would travel all over the world. We partied. I would get high off pills, and even do a line every now and then. I was partying so hard that I didn't have time for anything, including college. I didn't care that my parents extended the execution date of my trust fund so I wouldn't get it when I turned 18, because I was making money hustling. It was all just fun and games to me until I got jumped by some jealous hoodrats. Those chicks made me hustle a Rick Ross-looking dude and then they turned around and beat me down. I got beat so badly, I was in intensive care. The worst part was that the chicks set up the dude to make it look like he was the one that beat me up and he spent some time in jail over it.

After I left intensive care I quit hustling, but I continued partying and my drug use spiraled out of control. I used up all of my hustle money, my parents cut me off, and I was left with nothing until Logan swooped in and saved me. He put me in rehab and helped me get my life on track. Nonetheless, Logan knows all of this and he holds it over my head to control me. If he was to release this information to the media it would harm my family's business, because I was stealing the date rape drugs from our pharmaceutical company. Not only did I put the family business at risk, but criminal charges could be brought against me and Angel, as well. So I have always felt that I have no choice but to stay in this marriage to protect myself, but more importantly, my family.

Logan smiles at me and sticks his arm out for me to take. He escorts me to our car and opens the door for me to get in. He hops in the driver's side and we take off. Once we are out of our gated community, Logan's phone rings. It's hooked up to the car's speaker by Bluetooth and I can hear his mother's Southern accent snarling as soon as he answers.

"Logan, I will never know why you married that Yankee bitch. She's trying to keep me from my grandson and saying it's all your fault. But I know you wouldn't do anything like that, would you, Sweet Tea?"

Logan looks over at me with contempt in his eyes. "Of course not, Ma. You can see Ethan tomorrow."

"That's my boy. I'll talk to you later, son," Nancy says sweetly before hanging up.

My heart starts pounding. I can explain myself, but there's no point. Not taking his eyes off me, he asks, "You're trying to keep my mother away from *my* child?"

Logan drives through a red light as a car is approaching through the intersection. I hear its breaks screech to a halt before narrowly missing T-boning us. I feel like my heart just jumped through my chest. The vehicle's angry driver blasts his horn at us over and over again as we drive onto the highway.

"Keep your eyes on the road! What are you doing?" I shriek. He almost killed us. I begin to breathe heavily.

Logan turns his head to the road. He slams his foot on the gas pedal. The speedometer swings to the right. Fifty, seventy, ninety mph. My heart rate increases as the speed does. As our speed surges to 160 mph I scream at Logan again. "What are you doing? Slow down!" The hairs on the back of my neck stand up.

"You don't want my mother to see Ethan because you

are trying to leave me. I'll kill you. I'll kill us both before that happens. I'll drive this car off the road," Logan says with a sly grin. "Are you ready to die, Kylie?"

Anxiety runs through my veins as I sign the cross over my chest before gripping the door handle. I don't know what else to do, so I beg for my life. "I'm not trying to leave you. I'm not! Like you said, Nancy can see Ethan tomorrow. Slow down!"

Blue and red lights flash behind us and to my relief Logan pulls over to the side of the road and my breathing slows down. A police officer approaches us and Logan rolls the window down. The officer looks at Logan and his eyes widen with excitement.

"Are you Logan Beckham, quarterback for the Atlanta Nighthawks?" the officer asks, star struck.

Logan smiles. "Yes. That's me. Is there a problem, officer?"

"Oh, you were going a little over the speed limit. I'll let you go with a warning, but only this one time if you promise to demolish Maryland in next week's game."

"I'll certainly try my best. We spanked the dog pants off them last year. I think we can do it again this year."

"Can you sign this for my son? He loves you almost as much as me," he says, handing over his ticket pad and Logan signs it.

Fuming, my face flushes red. This is some bull. Logan should have been arrested for reckless driving. He almost killed me, himself, and any other person out on the road tonight, but because he knows how to throw a ball he's let go without a second thought.

Logan pulls off bragging about how big of a celebrity he is. He gushes about himself as if he didn't threaten to kill me a few moments ago. While he brags I sit quietly and

51

listen until we arrive at the gala.

Cameras are outside in full force as we walk hand in hand on the red carpet full of smiles, looking like America's favorite couple. We walk inside and I see the cast with the camera crew. This has been a horrible day and I don't feel like faking like my life is perfect. I put on my smiling mask and stroll over to the ladies.

"Stop and smell the Rose. I have arrived," I announce to the ladies.

"Yuck, is that what that smell is?" Skylar makes fun of me. This chick thinks she's a comedian.

I completely disregard Skylar, the "wife" I despise the most. She dates Blake Williams, who plays for the Atlanta Eagles, but she can't keep a man for nothing. I smile and greet Blake while still ignoring Skylar. Angel and I have a bet on how long it will take Blake to get tired of her. My bet is that he'll do it as soon as she is done filming the show. I'm sure he's using her to get a little shine on TV to help get him endorsements. Skylar is the ultimate groupie that goes from basketball player to basketball player until one takes pity and claims her. She probably has trouble keeping a man because she's a scandalous jerk. Remember the two jealous hoodrats I was talking about? The ones that forced me to hustle the Rick Ross lookalike and then put me in the hospital? She's one of them. She doesn't remember me, but I will never forget her.

Standing next to Skylar is her flunky, Gabrielle, or as she prefers to be called, Elle like the magazine. I give her a dry hello. She has striking high cheekbones, short dark hair, and is of British descent. She claims to be of royal blood, but chicks be out here lying for notoriety and fame. To say the least I don't care for her at all, mostly because she's Skylar's lackey. She was going by the nickname Gabby until Skylar told her to switch it up to Elle. She was sporting a lace front wig until Skylar told her to go short. Heck, if Skylar told her it was cool to have herpes she wouldn't hesitate to get infected. She's such a follower. I can't respect anyone who doesn't have a mind of their own.

As much as I don't like Elle, I have to give it to her for snagging one of the hottest men on earth, Isaque Melo. I look around for Isaque and he is nowhere to be found; probably mingling with the crowd looking for his next mistress. He's known to be flirtatious and when he speaks with that Brazilian accent women around the world swoon. She has been engaged to her soccer-playing boyfriend for about six years now. I don't think they will ever set a date, but even if it has been for fifty years, at least she is engaged, which is more than I can say about her supervisor Skylar, who will probably never marry. Like my sister Bella says, "Hoes don't get saved."

That brings me to Tori. She's totally a skank, but I totally love her. Most people assume her name is short for Victoria, but it is actually a Japanese name that means bird. She confided in me that her very strict parents are first generation immigrants from Japan and wanted her to have a Japanese name that would sound American at the same time. She rebels against her parents by exclusively dating, or more like having sex, with white guys and partying on a regular basis. She's just a fun chick and I love hanging out with her. Tori gives me a big hug and hands me a cocktail that I shouldn't be drinking as a recovering alcoholic.

Tori is most known for being arrested for having sex with a professional race car driver. After the stands were cleared out after he won a competition, they were caught by a security guard getting it *in* on the race track inside the winning car. The police recovered a surveillance tape of the whole freaky deed, and somehow it got leaked and it was eventually sold to a porn production company. Just scandalous. Her parents disowned her, but if it's any consolation she is still racking in big bucks from that tape five years later.

I smile hello at Jordyn and her husband, Antonio Lewis. They have been together since high school and are a super cute couple. They look so much alike that if I didn't know any better, I would think they were brother and sister. I would try to be Jordyn's friend if she wasn't so busy being up Skylar's behind. She's not a complete minion like Elle, however she has made it clear that her loyalties lie with Skylar.

Jordyn's gorgeous dark skin glows. I eye her coily, springy hair that falls down to her shoulders, wishing I could touch it. It's so pretty. But as interesting as her hair is, that is where all interest stops. Her personality is unremarkable and she's unmemorable. She's only on the show because she's friends with Skylar and her husband happens to be one of the best pitchers in baseball.

"I can't wait for you all to meet my sister, Angel Jones. She's on her way now," I tell the ladies. Skylar is looking like she is trying to put a face to the name.

"Skylar, I think you've met her before. Don't you know our older sister, Beau James?" I hide my satisfaction as I watch anger flash across Skylar's face. In my opinion, Beau basically stole Skylar's man, Israel James, star point guard for Indiana. Skylar was in a committed relationship with Israel when Beau swept in and got him to propose to her in less than six months. She knew what she wanted and she got it, and from what I've observed that's Beau's life motto. Beau gets what Beau wants. She wanted to be an attorney, she wanted to be a self-made millionaire, she wanted to be happy, and she wanted to be with the father of her children; and she got it, all of it. Maybe I should start taking notes.

Shannon pulls me off to the side. "Kylie, you just got here and you're already boring. What we filmed of you earlier today wasn't all that entertaining either."

"I was in my underwear. How was that boring?"

"You're just too nice. Viewers want to see an argument. To see you flip out on someone. Do something to turn up."

I hear Skylar mumbling something slick about Angel and I see Angel walk through the door. I quickly down the drink Tori gave me. "I just did," I tell Shannon, handing her my empty glass. I walk away to go hug Angel.

TESTIMONIAL

"Tell me how you really feel about your cast-mates." Shannon asks. "Don't hold back."

I begin by enthusing over my relationship with Angel. "Angel is my day one. I've known her since we were eleven and we moved down here to Atlanta together. She's the only person I know for sure that will have my back."

Shannon frowns at me. I guess she didn't like my happy-go-lucky response. "You have known Angel during her video vixen days. What do you think about her going from video hoe to wife?"

She thinks she's slick trying to bait me to say something crazy about Angel to put a riff in our friendship. She would love to capture that on camera. I smile, determined not to give her what she wants.

"Daniel is so lucky to have Angel in his life. I can't wait to welcome her into the wives club."

Shannon purses her lips. "What about Jordyn? I don't

think she likes you much," Shannon tries to provoke me.

"Jordyn who?" I stick my neck out, pretending like I was trying to hear her better.

"Jordyn Lewis. Medium height, dark-skinned black lady with curly hair," Shannon describes.

I roll my eyes. "Jordyn's a nothing. A nobody. Enough said. Moving on to something more relevant."

"And Tori? Don't you think she drinks too much?" Shannon baits.

"Tori knows how to toss one back, okay." I snap my fingers. "Her cure for a hangover is to just stay drunk. She definitely knows how to keep a party going," I giggle.

Shannon snickers before asking, "What did you think about Skylar's quip? She basically said you stank?"

"Skylar does a lot of smack talking to have so many skeletons in her closet. As far as I'm concerned, she's nothing more than a used condom ready to be discarded." I roll my neck.

"Yes, tell me more. I want to know about these skeletons," Shannon digs.

I raise an eyebrow. "All you need to know is if Skylar keeps messing with me I will be the Rose to put a thorn in that ass. Shit will get real."

"Juicy. Juicy. One more thing. Early today after we left did you put the spice back in the bedroom with your husband?"

I pause, contemplating how I want to answer. I don't want to piss Logan off. "You know the saying it's not the size of the ship but the motion in the ocean? Well Logan has a cruise ship too large to be at sea. He was definitely sailing it and sailing it well…" I pause and flash back to the drive to the gala. F it; after everything he put me through today. He won't see this until it airs. "… and then the ship sank. I would have been glad if it lasted more than two minutes. Does anyone have some blue pills we can borrow?"

6
Dirty Pasts on Red Carpets

Angel

Sexy and elegant all wrapped into one, I step out of the limo in a white strapless, floor-length Alexander McQueen gown with a sweetheart neckline. The dress clings to my body, showing off my svelte figure. I feel at home floating down the red carpet. Crazy how a week ago reporters didn't know my name, but now all I hear is "Angel, over here. Angel, can we get a word?" I keep my conversation very brief with reporters and smile while all the photographers snap pictures of me. The looks, the whispers, the compliments, I love it all. I have arrived. I giggle to myself. Not a movie shot or a magazine cover, yet I am on everyone's lips.

I sashay into the building still feeling like I'm the shit. That is, until Kylie brings me back to reality."

"Snap out of it. Damn, where were you, girl? I could see the stars in your eyes." I shake my head, laughing at Kylie, and then notice the dang on cameras for the show. I hope they didn't catch me having my moment.

"Hey, sexy. Look at you." I twirl Kylie around and she does the same to me.

"Look, I know you have to make appearances and be on Daniel's arm, but find me so I can introduce you to the rest of the girls."

"Yay, I can't wait," I give Kylie some side eye as sarcasm drips from my lips. I don't have a problem with meeting the other ladies, making friends, and playing nice. Well, with all of them except Skylar. I will never forget what that scandalous bitch did to my sisters and my niece and nephew. She almost ruined Beau and Kylie's lives. I know I am a good actress, but I am going to have one hell of a time trying to act nice to her and keep my hands from around her neck.

Kylie and I kiss each other's cheeks before disappearing into a sea of pretty faces, fine men, and millions of dollars' worth of bling. I make it to the front of the room and try to pass Mr. Silver who is sitting at the main table along with Mrs. Silver. She stands up to give me a hug and her red sequined dress pricks my skin. She holds me tight for a moment and I enjoy the embrace. Once she releases me she looks me up and down and smiles. "I love you, sweetheart." She rubs my cheek and hugs me again. I think she knows what Dennis said to Daniel; she must. She has always been nice to me but tonight it feels different.

"I love you too," I say, smiling curiously at her. I want to talk to her. I want to know how she feels about what her husband said. I wonder how she could love and stay married to that ignorant man for all these years. She is so warm and inviting to me but Dennis is still ice cold.

"Hi, Angel. You look lovely." Dennis stands up to give me a hug. This time my embrace is just as cold as his. I have no desire to be fake, but I was raised to respect my elders, so that is what I do.

"Thank you." I squeeze the words through my tight lips and a fake smile.

"Wow." Daniel takes me into his arms. His hazel eyes look golden under the bright lights. "You are so gorgeous," he says, beaming.

"Stop." I turn away from him, embarrassed and blushing. He is saying all this in front of the Mayor, the whole Atlanta Eagles squad, and tons of other celebrities and reporters.

"You do, Angel, and your idea about having celebrities donate items for the auction is brilliant." Daniel continues to beam.

We sit at our table and make small talk as comedian Kenny Love, the gala MC, tells jokes and auctions off items.

"Wow, Dennis Silver is auctioning his suite for the regular season. Are you gon' be there, too?" Kenny and everyone else's eyes focus on Dennis waiting for a response.

"Of course. Where else would I be?" he chuckles.

"Okay, okay. So I was thinking who will be the most interesting person to be in the suite with you." Kenny pauses and starts scanning the room. A spotlight appears and seems to be following his eyes. Kenny and the spotlight focus on Revis Johnson, star player for the Atlanta Eagles.

"Revis, maybe you can sit up there."

Revis looks confused about the comment.

"I mean, you not doing much on the court these days. You might as well sit it out and watch how the real players play. You and Dennis can go over your contract or something."

The audience erupts into laughter and after looking embarrassed for a couple of seconds, Revis yells out, "Forget you, shorty. You better check my stats."

The 6'8" point guard stands up, poking his chest out. Everyone starts cheering. Revis is right. He led the team to the Eastern Conference semi-finals and yeah, they got knocked out by Indiana, but they did well, especially since they have such a young team. Revis is only 22 years old. He led the league in triple doubles and was even nominated for MVP.

"It's alright Revis, just playing. Congrats on the season. Anyway I am sure I can find someone much more interesting to be in the suite with Dennis Silver. Any suggestions?" Kenny holds out his mic and people start blurting out ridiculous suggestions.

"Likki 3Ways," I blurt out, catching Kenny Love's attention.

Waves of laughter flood the room. Likki is a female rapper from Atlanta. Provocative, sexy, and controversial are just a few words that can describe her. I guess I think she is the one person in the room that would make Dennis the most uncomfortable. She is short and petite with cocoa skin that is awkwardly contrasted with a pink lace front wig. Her short, tight Versace dress has every last one of her curves about to burst out. She stands up and starts dancing her way to the front of the room.

"What made you think of her?" Daniel whispers in my ear, grinning from ear to ear. I can tell he is getting just as much pleasure out of this as me. Dennis looks over his shoulder as the rapper dances closer and closer to him. His face turns red from embarrassment and I can tell he is uncomfortable.

"Hey Dennis, promise I can sit on your lap if I get the seats?" Likki rubs her hand over Dennis' bald head and he flinches. I giggle to myself, very pleased with his reaction.

"Alright, let the bidding begin at $3,000," Kenny announces.

"$5,000," an older gentleman at the main table speaks up. He's probably one of Dennis' friends who shares the same beliefs as him and wants to save him from being uncomfortable.

"$10,000," Likki shouts, sitting her tush on the table right next to Dennis. Mrs. Silver looks about as amused as me as Dennis tries to scoot his chair away from Likki.

"Hold on, baby, don't get nervous. Once I get those suite seats we gon' be spending a lot of time together."

"$20,000," the older gentlemen shouts again, sounding irritated.

"$50,000," Likki leans over to get a good look at the older gentlemen.

"Wow, $50,000! Likki, I didn't know you were a basketball fan." Kenny smiles.

"Nah, I'm a Dennis Silver fan!" Likki crosses her legs and rubs Dennis' back. I couldn't have scripted this better. I hope the TV cameras are catching every minute of this. I am enjoying watching Dennis squirm in his chair.

"$50,000 going once...twice..." Kenny begins a countdown. I glance over at the older gentlemen. He is sitting there turning red, I think more from anger than embarrassment, but he doesn't up the bid.

"$100,000!" I finally yell, deciding that God would probably want me to put Mr. Silver out of his misery. I think I'm doing it even more for Likki. I want to save her from having to deal with a whole season of Dennis Silver and his friends.

"Yeah, I don't like you that much," Likki hops off the table and bends over, giving Dennis a big wet kiss on his cheek before heading towards her seat.

"Can I borrow your fiancée for a minute?" Kylie gives Daniel a hug before tapping my shoulder, eyeing me.

"I won't be long, babe," I stand up to follow Kylie so she can introduce me to the other cast mates.

"Be on your best behavior," Daniel says, smiling nervously.

I told Daniel about how Skylar tried to sabotage Real and Beau's relationship, but I never discussed how she

63

almost got Kylie killed. I feel anger rising inside of me as Kylie and I walk towards a lounge area right outside of the ladies' restroom. Kylie seems cool, though. Maybe she has forgiven Skylar. She opens the door to the lounge and I am immediately bombarded with the scents of all types of expensive perfumes. Three beautiful women and Skylar's punk self are standing in front of me.

Kylie gives a quick introduction of each of the wives and girlfriends. Tori, with a wine glass in her hand, hugs me and tells me how nice it is to finally meet me. "Kylie has told us so much about you. Wow, you are gorgeous," she compliments.

The other two wives, Elle and Jordyn hug me loosely and quickly with little smirks on their faces. Looks like they have already taken sides. Skylar just stands with a mug on her face. I stare back, not the least bit intimidated by her. I know she is weak and pathetic, and she is obviously holding some harsh feelings for me. The feeling is absolutely mutual.

"Hope you are not like your sister, taking women's men and ruining people's relationships," Skylar finally speaks, rolling her eyes.

"You gotta be kidding me. You want to talk about breaking up relationships? You almost ruined two children's lives. You scandalous conniving—"

"Shut up! Shut up! Shut up!" Skylar yells, cutting me off. "Don't fuck with me!" she screams, walking up on me.

"I promise I will finish what my sister started," I clinch my fists tightly, waiting for her to get within arm's reach.

"Ladies!" Security quickly swarms us, standing between Skylar and me as she spews profanities.

"Enough, ladies!" Evan's voice booms over the chaos. "Let's call it a night. I think we have enough footage for tonight. Go enjoy yourselves." Everyone disperses and he walks over to me. "We need to get another shot with Dennis since you won the bid.

"I need a minute, Evan," I say dismissively as I walk into the bathroom.

I play back what just happened in my mind. I shouldn't have provoked Skylar. I hope I don't embarrass Daniel. God, I am trying to do better. I really am. But it is hard and she came for me first. I try to reason with God, but I know I could have handled things differently. It's not like I didn't know I would have to be around her when I agreed to do the show. God help me tame my tongue and my anger. Psalms 18:21 comes to mind. *Death and life are in the power of the tongue.*

I take a paper towel and lightly wipe my face, making sure not to mess up my makeup. I still have to go back to the main table and smile like everything is okay. I take a deep breath and head out of the bathroom.

"Prayer, patience, preparation," I repeat the 3 Ps GG taught me. I don't know how they can help me right now, but they are stuck in my head.

"Que pasa?" I feel a strong grip on my arm and a deep voice asking me what's up. I feel my heart pounding in my chest. Oh my God, Alejandro sent one of his guys here. I turn around to face a medium height Latino man with short hair and sexy bedroom eyes staring at me like he wants to kill me.

"Donde esta Alejandro?" I ask him about Alejandro.

"Quién es Alejandro? Otro hombre le roban?" he asks if Alejandro is another guy I've robbed.

His words catch me off guard. *Some other guy I robbed.* Oh my God, he must be an old mark. I have hustled so many men I don't remember their faces, but he obviously remembers me.

"Que deseas?" I ask him what he wants. I don't have time to get caught talking secretively to some man.

"Dinero. $15,000 you took from me," he says, raising his voice. I feel his grip getting tighter on my arm.

I look down at his left hand, hoping to see a wedding band. I don't, but most men bring their wives or significant other to these events, so I try to call him out, praying that it works.

"Donde esta tu esposa?" I ask him about his wife. His eyes widen.

"Bitch."

"Cabron!" we exchange insults. "So you can either go back in there to your wife and forget me or you can stay out here and try to extort money out of me, but I wonder how you're going to explain this to her." I am hoping he cares more about his wife than money.

"What would your rich white man say if he knew you were a thief?" he counters.

"Let's go see." I pull away from him and head towards the main room, trying to call his bluff. I catch a glimpse of Kylie walking towards the back of the building. I want to make a beeline to go talk to her about what has just happened. We talked about what we would do if we ever ran into one of our old marks, but never thought it would actually happen.

Something seems up with Kylie as she tiptoes past me without even looking my way. Her eyes are straight forward. I wonder if another mark, maybe the one that was with this guy, found her. I decide not to follow after Kylie. She can handle herself. I don't want this asshole following me and trying to hem me up again.

I walk through the door without looking back. *God,*

please don't let him be following me. I smile as I head back to the table.

"So Blake, you a housewife now?" I hear Kenny making jokes about Blake and his slutty girlfriend, Skylar.

"Nah, but my girl is," Blake says defensively.

"Your girl looks familiar," Kenny says, making eye contact with Skylar.

"Did we date or something?" Kenny asks as the crowd erupts into laughter.

As I stroll by Blake's table I mutter under my breath, "Probably."

I catch Blake and Skylar mugging me. I ignore them and take my seat next to my love.

"What happened?" Daniel whispers in my ear as I sit down.

"What? What are you talking about?" I nervously ask. Did he see me out there with that guy? What is he thinking? I have to think of something to tell him. *He thought he knew me. He tried to flirt with me.* I try to quickly think of a lie. I start scanning the room for the old mark. I spot him staring hard three tables behind me. I feel my heart still racing. He turns away and my jaw just about drops when I see him kiss Elle.

"With the other ladies. Are you okay?" Daniel gets my attention. I am sure my emotions are written all over my face.

"You know what? We will talk about that later. It was crazy. Security and producers had to get involved. Shoot, I forgot, they want me to shoot a scene with your father. Babe, I am going to do that and then head home. I have a migraine. You don't mind, do you?" I give my best innocent damsel face.

"You want me to go with you?"

"No, stay and enjoy yourself. This is your night."

"I love you."

"I love you so much." I kiss Daniel deeply and patiently. I really do love him so much and I am not going to let my past dirt ruin my future. I put on a smile and mentally prepare myself to pretend that I'm enthused that Dennis Silver will be a new addition to my family.

TESTIMONIAL

"Never ceases to amaze me how people want to throw dirt on somebody while forgetting about their own flaws," I immediately start in on Skylar. "I could annihilate her if I chose to but it's not in me." My eyes get bigger and I purse my lips while moving my head side to side as I stare into the camera. I taunt the camera, knowing someday Skylar will see this.

I can hear the producers asking me for more information. I don't know if I have ever despised someone to the point of hate but that is how I feel about Skylar. Just thinking about her makes me cringe. I feel my hands gripping my dress tightly as I ball a fist.

"Elaborate more on your history and beef with Skylar," I hear Evan say in the background. I bet they would like that and I am almost tempted to. I can't talk about how she almost beat Kylie to death, because that could implicate all my sisters and me in the hustle and ruin all of our lives. Skylar's deceptions and treachery almost ruined the twins' lives, too. What she did to them, shoot, I almost think it is more scandalous than the Kylie beat down. Skylar was so determined to keep Real, she was willing to risk the happiness and relationship my niece and nephew have with their father. I still remember my sister crying over her children's pain, because they thought their daddy didn't love them anymore. My sisters and I, myself especially, know how it feels to grow up without a father and Skylar didn't give a damn about anything or anyone but herself.

"Ask Skylar. She knows what she's done," I reply, standing up and walking out of the room.

7
Restricted Access

Kylie

RESTRICTED flashes across the caller ID. I smile and answer. "Same time, same place." I keep it short and don't wait for a response before hanging up.

Ethan presses a button on his Touch and Teach Turtle. The toy lights up and says. "D is for dog."

Ethan lights up as bright as the turtle and points towards his stuffed dog lying on the floor across the room.

"Dog, Mommy, dog!" I may be biased but my child is brilliant.

"Yes, sweetie. That is a dog. And what sounds do dogs make?" I ask my son.

Ethan begins to bark as his father walks in the room and scoops him up from the floor. "I'm about to leave for the game," he announces. "You're coming, right?"

"I have to film today. I probably won't get home until really late. I'm supposed to meet the girls for a late lunch then do a night cap at Jordyn's," I remind Logan and he silently nods his head. He kisses Ethan before placing him in my arms and then kisses me goodbye on the forehead.

"Get 'em, babe. Beat Maryland," I encourage Logan as he walks out the door. Before he shuts the door he sticks his head back in.

"You should have the nanny bring Ethan to the game."

"Whatever you wish, honey." Of course he wants his sidepiece at the game if I'm not going to be there. I'm all for it if that is why he has been so calm lately. Logan and I have been on good terms. He hasn't been violent towards me all week, but then again I've been walking on eggshells trying not to piss him off. It's been peaceful and I'm grateful for it.

******

Time flies as I play with Ethan for a while. When it gets close to kick off for Logan's game, I instruct Logan's sidepiece to escort my son to his game per his wishes before heading out to our five-car garage. I slip on my shades and walk pass the Bentley, the Porsche, and the BMW, jetting straight to the Jeep. I forego the flash for what I'm about to do. I need to be low-key. I drive across the city from John's Creek to a hotel in Marietta, my discrete meeting spot. No one recognizes me here or even cares who I am. I'm just another regular white girl, which is exactly what I'm going for.

When I arrive at the hotel, I go straight to the room. No need to check in. It's the same suite every month. Once a month I get a call from RESTRICTED and I'm off to a mini vacay to forget about my worries, except for last month when I was too busy to get away. As usual, I see the security latch on the door sticking out and holding the door slightly open.

I walk inside and spot a silver gun with a black handle lying next to the flat screen TV playing the Atlanta vs. Maryland football game. I stop to watch Logan do what he does best. Logan is waiting for his receivers to get in place and he is bulldozed by Maryland's defense. I smirk. Logan peels himself off the field. This time when the defense attacks he runs. Dashing 18 yards down the field into the end zone, he's untouchable. He scores a touchdown.

"And that's why I was able to sign him to a $120 million contract," Mario beams, sprawled across the bed naked. He knows that's my favorite outfit on him. I admire

72

his body as he licks his lips and blows me a kiss. I reminisce on how those lips were licking the lips between my legs at the gala last week. Mario was just holding my starving body over until today, for the main course.

"And you still owe me a piece of your commission. I was the one that convinced my husband to hire you as his agent," I joke. "What's 10% of 10%?"

Mario smiles and turns off the TV. I motion for him to come to me. He obeys and slides off the bed. He lifts my shirt over my head, then slips my breast from the cup of my bra and massages my nipple. I push him on the bed.

"Do you know how much I love you?" Mario leans up on his forearms.

I slip off my jeans and panties.

"Mmm." He licks his lips, his eyes admiring my Brazilian wax. He loves it when I wax the fuzz from my peach. I lightly push him again, knocking him off his forearms.

"Shhhh." I mount his face so he can't talk. I don't want to talk about love right now; I just want to make love. I've been waiting for this for over a month. I rub his Caesar haircut as I slowly rock my hips back and forth, stopping only when his face is covered in my peach juice. I begin to lift up and he pulls me down. I smack his hand and giggle.

"Stop it!"

I sit on his pleasure stick and glide up and down on it. He cups my girls like he is holding on for the ride of his life. I lean forward and kiss him intensely. We take turns sucking each other's tongues before I pull my kisses away. Without getting off his pleasure stick I spin around and ride him reverse-cowgirl style. I pretend like I'm dancing to Ciara singing about promises and I wiggle and slow grind like she does in the video. I grab his arms, cueing him to sit up and he obliges. By the way he's groaning and his toes are curling I can tell he's ready to explode inside me, but he's not a selfish lover. He won't cum until I do. He reaches his fingers down to my peach and strokes my pleasure button.

My body begins to jerk uncontrollably.

"I love you. Jesus. I love you!" I feel a gush of man juice flow into me. He came but he keeps going; keeps bouncing me up and down on his lap. His appetite for my peach never ceases to amaze me. I never knew a man could have multiple orgasms until I met him. He will go all night if I let him, but the orgasm he gave me was strong and I am done. I don't have it in me to go another round. I push myself off of him and fall to the bed. My chest is heaving up and down as I try to catch my breath. He falls to the bed behind me and we spoon.

"You ready to talk?" Mario asks, breaking the silence.

"No." I focus my attention on our interlocking fingers and the contrasting colors of our ebony and ivory skin.

"Bae, I'm serious. I love you. We can't go on like this," he pleads as I get up and go to the shower. I really don't want to hear what he has to say right now. He follows behind me, standing on the other side of the closed door. "I'm tired of being your best kept secret."

I laugh. I didn't mean to; it just came out. If he only knew my real best kept secret he probably wouldn't love me anymore. If he knew how I used to drug and rob men he would go running in the other direction.

With frustration in his voice, he says, "He doesn't treat you like I will. The fact that you are here with me proves that." He gets silence in return for his pleading. I hear him walk away. I finish my shower and get dressed. His plea for me to leave my husband begins again. He is

74

leaning on a pillow with his tablet in his lap.

"Marry me."

I laugh in Mario's face. I can't take him seriously. He looks at me, unpleased that I find his marriage proposal humorous. I walk over to him and gently kiss him on the lips.

"I love you, but I'm not leaving my family for you. I'm Catholic so if my marriage doesn't work out, I will never remarry." Now it's Mario's turn to be silent. "You know this from the last five times you proposed to me. I don't know why you're acting surprised like you don't know what's up."

"So it's against your religion to marry me, but it's okay to fuck me, commit adultery, cum all over my dick, and tell me how much you love me?" he asks in a cynical voice.

"Exactly. I'm glad you understand," I change the subject, trying not to reveal my cards to Mario. I don't want to tell him that I wish I met him first, how even though I'm not getting a divorce I have plans to shut down my husband's abusive ways, or how I can never trust another man. I glance at Mario's tablet and see he is watching something on Netflix. "What are you watching? A documentary on how to jack off?" I joke.

"Nah, with you I don't need that. I'm watching *House of Cards*. It's about this cutthroat dude named Frank Underwood who is basically a puppet master getting everyone to do and believe exactly what he wants. He's such a mastermind that he became president of the country without a single vote. I wish I could Frank Underwood myself to the top of my career," he says, using Frank Underwood as a verb.

I wonder if he is trying to Frank Underwood me for my money like Logan did or if he really loves me like he says he does.

"Frank Underwood, huh? Well I have a scene to shoot, so I gotta go." I kiss him and walk out of the room.

I go home and quickly change clothes and cars before Logan gets there. I don't want anyone to see me arrive on set in the same Jeep that I drove to the hotel. In fact, I bought the Jeep solely to drive myself to my little escapes. I never drive anywhere else in it.

I slide into the BMW and drop the top before cruising to Chop Lobster Bar, a swank restaurant in Buckhead. When I arrive, I spot Skylar, Jordyn, and Elle seated at the outdoor tables already filming. Damn, neither Angel nor Tori is here. After what happened last week I already know this is about to be some bull. I bet Shannon showed them the testimonial of me talking smack about them and they want to confront me. I turn on my perky face and hop out the car. The ladies see me walking towards them and they hush their conversation. I sit down and focus on the scowl on Skylar's face.

I skip the pleasantries.

"Where's Angel and Tori?"

"I-D-K. How am I supposed to know where sluts go during the daytime?" Skylar snarls at me.

"Really? Can I at least order a drink before you start yappin' at the mouth?" I ask Skylar. I see Jordyn out of the corner of my eye reaching for her drink like she's going to toss it on me. The producers must have been in her ear telling her how boring she is. So to get more camera time she thinks she's about to toss a drink on me. I don't think so; I'm not having it.

I snatch the glass from her hand and smash it on the ground.

"Don't even try it. You are not about to throw anything

at me." I wave my finger in Jordyn's face.

Jordyn pushes my finger out of her face. "Well you said you wanted a drink. I was trying to help you out."

Elle butts in, "Kylie, you're so classless. I guess money can't buy etiquette."

Skylar smirks. "All I want to know is why in the world would you bring your hoe ass friend into our circle? I saw Angel all over Isaque at the gala."

"Lies you tell. I don't believe that for one second," I say with attitude.

"I heard Isaque mention something about $15,000. What is that? Cash for ass?" Skylar quips.

I don't bother to address Skylar and her lies. I look Elle in the eyes.

"Skylar is not your friend. She is your ringleader and misery loves company. Keep listening to Misery over here and she will destroy your relationship so you can be just as miserable as her. Unlike Skylar, you have a man who actually loves you and isn't pretending so that he can be on TV. Stand up to Skylar and get a mind of your own. You got that, Gabby?"

Elle is silent and looks like she is actually contemplating the point I just made, even though she turns up her nose at the mention of her former nickname.

The next thing I know I hear a bunch of fuck yous, hoes, and bitches coming out of Skylar's mouth. Soon after, Elle joins in with Skylar like the follower she is, too blind to see the truth for what it is. Angel doesn't want her man. I bet Skylar made up the whole story to put dirt on Angel's name. And Jordyn just sits there quietly like the lame that she is, undoubtedly afraid to say or do anything to me after I smashed that glass. I hope I put enough fear in her that I will embarrass her on national TV.

77

"On that note I'm done with you three stooges. Larry, Curly, and Moe, call me when you get some sense." I nod my head at each of them as I say the Stooges' names. I stand up and go to my car, turning on *My Songs Know What You Did In The Dark* by Fall Out Boy. Before I pull off, Shannon flags me down smiling, no doubt because she just got a juicy scene that she can sensationalize.

"What?" I bark at Shannon.

"We need to shoot your testimonial," she reminds me.

"I'm not about to do that shit right now," I snap at Shannon. I know she set me up to be blindsided by Skylar and her cronies and her face is the last thing I want to see right now.

"That's okay. We still have other things to shoot today. We can do it tomorrow. Are you sure you don't want to have a night cap at Jordyn's?"

I'm not about to do that shit either. I crank up the volume on my stereo, rev the engine, and pull off without saying another word to Shannon.

On my way home, my phone starts buzzing. Bella's name is on the caller ID. I hit the ignore button and call Angel. I haven't talked to her since the gala and I need to give her a heads up. She answers and tells me she is leaving a movie audition. I don't mean to cut her off, but I need to spill the tea.

"Girl, let me tell you what just went down. I wish...I wish you were there. These chicks blindsided me and they are trying to set you up," I say, slamming my hand on the steering wheel. I give Angel the blow by blow of everything that just happened. Angel tells me that Isaque was an old mark and gives me all the details about what actually happened at the gala. I pull up to my house as Angel is finishing up her story. I see a familiar car in the driveway—Mario's. I thought Logan already signed his contract, but I guess there are some loose ends that need to be tied up.

"Aye, I have to go," I say, hanging up the phone with Angel. I park and walk inside. This is about to be completely awkward, but facing my husband and my lover in the same room isn't anything I haven't done before.

I walk into the kitchen. No one. I walk into the great room. No one. I walk into the billiard room. No one. Maybe Mario came over and they went to a restaurant to go talk business. I climb the stairs and go to Ethan's room. He's not there and there is no sign of the nanny. Yeah, everyone's gone. I'm about to jump in the shower then lie in bed and watch Frank Underwood on Netflix.

I take off my blouse and start stripping for my shower as I walk into my room. My husband is laying on his stomach under the covers making love faces and my lover is on top of him grunting as he thrusts, rocking the bed back and forth.

"What the…?!" I squeal.

Mario jumps up. He looks embarrassed as he quickly grabs his clothes and begins to get dressed.

"What is going on here? I don't understand." I look at Mario confused and hurt. He doesn't say anything. He just jets out of the room and I hear his car screech off.

I start to feel sick to my stomach.

"Are you gay? You're gay. You are gay!" I accuse Logan. Logan storms towards me butt naked and slams me to the floor.

"Shut up. Shut up! Don't you ever say that again. Shut up!" he screams.

TESTIMONIAL

"Did this chick just use text talk when speaking out loud? This is why I can't deal with simple bitches," I say, referring to Skylar's 'IDK' comment.

"Do you think Jordyn was really trying to throw her glass at you?" Shannon asks.

"I don't know," I say, waving my fingers towards the camera. "And I don't know what Jordyn thinks this is but I am not the one. Don't let my bank account fool you. I'm not above defending myself."

"Elle called you classless—"

"Forget Gabby," I say, cutting Shannon off. "They were definitely trying to set me up, but I'm classless? Get out of here with that." I flick my wrist as I turn my head away from the camera as if I'm over it.

"So let's get down to the meat of it. Skylar is making some serious accusations about your bestie."

"Why does Skylar even care? It's not her husband. If she stops using her vagina as community property then maybe she can get one. Let's compare Isaque's stats to Daniel's stats. Daniel is taller, looks better, and has more money."

"Sounds like you have a crush on somebody," Shannon taunts.

I whip my head at her and squint my eyes. "Let's not go there." Shannon really wants me to snap on her.

"Speaking of money, Skylar said Angel was trying to exchange her services for $15,000."

"Does Angel look like she needs $15,000? She's been flossing Berkin bags and Maseratis since she was sixteen. She got money on top of money and so does her future husband. Skylar's just mad because she's never seen $15,000 in her life. Instead of hating she needs to get like us."

"And what exactly does 'like us' mean?" Shannon antagonizes me.

"Rich, bitch!"

8
With So Much Drama in the ATL

Angel

My head is banging when I wake up. I don't know when Daniel got in but he is already up. I sit up and notice that all I have on is my bra and panties. My hair is smashed to my face and my mouth tastes like early morning breath and vodka and tonic. I lie back on the bed and close my eyes. I wish I could just crawl back under the covers and go to sleep. A week or two ago I could have, but my life has quickly turned from peaceful bliss to utter chaos.

Ever since Daniel took over ownership of the team, it seems like we are out at an event every night. I hear Beyoncé singing *Get Me Bodied*. It's my alarm. I have an audition for a role in an indie film about a struggling model who still lives in the 'hood—Decatur—and sells drugs to survive until she gets her big break. I thought the song was befitting given the character.

I hop in the shower and wash my hair. I don't have enough time to flat iron it out, so I am going curly. I throw on some dark blue skinny jeans and a cream knitted halter-top with six-inch nude pumps. The outfit accentuates my curves and the heels are one of my highest pairs. I am not short but I'm not model tall either. I am 5'5", so the heels help me look a lot taller.

I walk down to Mamá's room to discuss her current situation. I knock on her door. I am going to return the drugs and money to Alejandro and explain Mamá's fragile mental state. If he has any compassion whatsoever, he will take his stuff back and let my mother move on with her life. If sympathy doesn't work maybe more money will. I have

$2.2 million saved and one thing I know about people with money is that they rarely turn down more money.

After a few moments with no response, I knock on the door again.

"Mamá , what are you doing in there?" Again, no answer.

Please tell me this woman did not leave. I head downstairs. Why would she leave? If Alejandro finds her there is no telling what he will do to her or me. What if he finds out I lied to him? I panic.

Once downstairs, I smell the aroma of migas de arepa. I don't have a lot of good memories of her, but breakfast in the morning is one that I do have. She would always cook breakfast for me no matter what; I could depend on it.

"Hola, mija," Mamá calls out to me as I walk into the kitchen. "Que linda. Where are you going looking so cute?" She smiles at me.

I have dreamt of this moment; seeing my mom, talking to her, and eating her food, but I never thought it would happen.

"Babe, you didn't tell me your mom is such a great cook," Daniel says through a mouthful of food. I didn't notice him until now. "I bet that is where you get your cooking skills. Mrs. Jimenez, Angel is an excellent cook."

Daniel looks over at my mom smiling. I don't have the heart to tell him the truth, at least not right now when everything seems so perfect, but actually my GG and my sister Beau taught me how to cook.

"Mamá, yo quiero un poco por favor." I sit at the island next to Daniel and let her know I only want a little to eat.

"No, comer mucho Angel. No he cocinado para tu en mucho tiempo."

She is trying to stuff my face since I haven't had her cooking in a long time.

"I have an audition in about an hour. I can't eat a lot. Maybe you can fix dinner tonight?"

"Okay, that sounds great."

"Mamá, why don't you head upstairs to my closet so we can find you some clothes?"

"Okay," she says, excusing herself.

"Isn't it weird she didn't bring any clothes?" Daniel asks after she is out of the room.

"Oh, I forgot to tell you the airline lost her luggage," I lie to him quickly. It comes so natural and easy to me but I hate doing it to Daniel.

"How long is she going to be staying with us?"

"I don't know. I mean I didn't ask her. If it's a—"

"No, no. I was just thinking if she is going to be here for a while you two should go shopping so she can get some new clothes."

"Okay. I'll ask her," I state, standing up to leave.

"No kiss?" Daniel pulls me onto his lap. He wraps his arms around me and we just sit for a while staring into each other's eyes. I know he is the one. I have never worried about him cheating, lying, or hurting me and I don't know too many women who can make that claim. I press my lips up against Daniel's and then our tongues start to tango. I rub my fingers through his hair. I feel his piece up against my butt and I can't lie, I start to get aroused. Daniel slides his hand up my shirt and starts massaging my breasts.

"I gotta go, love," I say, hopping off his lap.

We have never had sex. Yes, I know it sounds crazy. Nine months of dating and no sex. Of the many things I have learned from my sisters the most important is no sex before marriage. I admire how Bella held on to her

85

virginity until she married the love of her life. And then there is Beau. Don't get me wrong, I love my niece and nephew so much but they are the perfect birth control. A one night stand almost ruined her life. I can remember plenty of conversations Beau and Bella had about how much she loves the twins but was so stressed about her situation.

"Come on!" I hear Daniel yell as I switch away. I can feel his eyes glued to my butt. It's not funny, but I can't help but to giggle. I know he wants to make love to me and I have found myself weak at times, especially after a few drinks. Just thinking about making love to him gets me wet. We haven't set a wedding date yet. I do want a big wedding, a white flowing gown and train, doves and stuff, however, I'd marry him tomorrow at the Justice of the Peace if he asked. I just want to be happy in love.

"Mamá, are you doing?" I walk into my closet and see her frantically going through my shoe boxes and drawers.

"Looking for some clothes," she anxiously replies.

"Okay. Well since I know where everything is let me help."

I escort her out of the closet and ask her to have a seat on the chaise. I can only image what is going through her head right now. She has basically decided to start a new life with nothing. I walk out of the closet with two options; a maxi dress, and a pair of casual linen slacks with a loose, flowing tank.

"Where is the stuff, Angel?"

"I have it somewhere safe. Mamá, don't worry about it. I have a plan, too. I am going to take the drugs and the money and give it back to Alejandro. I am going to call him and make arrangements today."

"What?! No! Are you crazy? I will not let you get any

more involved in this than you already are. I will do it. Now go get the stuff."

"No. He is very pissed with you and I am worried about what he might do to you if he sees you. You have to stay away from him."

"Angel!"

"There is nothing else to talk about," I say, walking out of my room and heading to hers to find where she hid Alejandro's money. She is fast on my heels. I don't understand what she is thinking. Meeting up with Alejandro could mean her life. I know Alejandro is getting older, probably pushing 60, but men like him do not deal well with betrayal and people who steal. Taking something from a drug lord is asking for trouble. Once in her room, I look through a few drawers and then under her bed, where I find the money.

"Angel, what are you doing?" Mamá, angrily asks. She drops the clothes on the floor and thrusts herself at me, trying to take the bag of money out of my hands.

"No, Mamá, what are you doing? If you are worried that you won't have enough money to start over, don't. I will give you money. How much is this?" I shake the bag. "$50,000? 100,000? Don't worry. I will go to the bank today and get you $100,000—"

"Cash," she cuts me off.

"Umm, no. How about a cashier's check? Mamá, I told you I will take care of you and I meant it."

I kiss her forehead then walk out of her room tightly gripping the bag of money. Once back in my closet, I take the drugs out of their hiding place and put them and the money into a little safe I keep hidden in the closet behind my clothes. I don't feel like I can trust that she won't try to get it and take it to Alejandro. I can understand her being worried about me, but I feel like I am the best and only shot at making things right with Alejandro. I leave for my audition with a million things running through my head.

* * * * *

"Angel Jimenez-Jones," a tall, slim chocolate woman steps out of a door and calls my name.

I walk past scowling faces and mean mugs from other chicks auditioning for a role in the movie too. I am sure they are little intimidated that I came with my own camera crew. The show is filming my audition. I am excited but also nervous because whether I do good or bad this will be played out on the show for the whole world to see.

However, I know I'm 'bout to kill it. *"How I know? I got a feeling."* I sing Kanye and Jay-Z's lyrics from *Niggas in Paris* in my head and I do my best Naomi Campbell walk into the audition room. The room is empty except for a table, the director, producer, and Nicole Wells, the woman that called for me. She wrote the script. I hand them my headshot and resume.

"Start when you're ready," Nicole says smiling at me. She has flawless mocha skin, high cheek bones, and big, full lips. Maybe this is a true story of her life. I feel even more motivated to do my best. I run my lines and it's a scene where the main character almost gets caught selling drugs to another model.

"That was great. Thank you. We will call you if you get the part." Nicole smiles once more when I am finished. She escorts me to the door and calls out the next girl's name. I feel confident in what I did. I tried my best to embody the character. I could feel her plight and honesty. The main character Erica is a hustla' just like me and my sisters, so I can relate.

As I walk out I see a tall light-skinned chick looking

me up and down. She looks familiar. I don't want to stare, but I am trying to put a name to the face. She is taller than me and very thin with huge, unnatural-looking breasts; she looks like she might tip over if she bends her head. Oh well, I can't remember who she is. I keep walking.

"Wow, Angel, you did great. I am sure you will get the part," Evan walks up and congratulates me.

"Yeah, I bet you will." The light-skinned chick whose name I can't recall walks over to Evan and me. I can hear shade all in her voice.

"Excuse me?" I cut my eyes over at her.

"Angel. I knew you looked familiar. Video hoe turned housewife and actress. Guess you turned that stereotype on its head. You know, *can't turn a hoe to a housewife*." She rolls her eyes.

There it is. The way she said hoe. How it rolled off her lips with such anger. Traci. All I remember is her first name. She is a for real video hoe. While I got my video parts based on my looks and personality, chicks like Traci often slept with rappers and directors in order to get parts.

I remember my first video when I was sixteen. It was after a wild party I threw at the condo with Young Will that Bella almost killed me over. I tried out for his video, *Money Hungry*.

"Yo, Billi!" Young Will yelled out the nickname he gave me when I walked into the audition room. I was shocked that he remembered me. I got the part in his video and played the main chick. In the video I ran a brothel full of grimy girls down to do whatever to get paid. Traci was one of them. The other girls and I wore tight little dresses, bikinis, and high heels—the typical wardrobe for video vixens. I wore a short fur vest in one scene. It was real chinchilla and Young Will let me have it after the shoot.

That pissed Traci off, since she was banging Young Will at the time. Afterwards, Young Will booked me for another video, then another, and another. He even recommended me to other people in the industry, which made her even more jealous.

"Hoe, stay away from Will!" Traci yelled at me backstage one day after a video shoot. I didn't get a chance to explain that nothing was going on with Will because she tried to step to me. I smushed her in her face and she fell out of her heels and onto the ground. The heckles and laughs filled the room, embarrassing her. When Traci tried to jump up and come for me again Young Will stopped her. I hadn't seen or thought about her since that day, but she obviously is still holding resentment towards me.

"You two know each other?" Evan asks, backing up and motioning for the camera guy to start rolling. I am sure Evan and whoever else is watching can peep the tension.

"Yeah, I know her scandalous ass," Traci quickly replies. "Like I said, she was a video hoe."

"Look, you can get out of here with that. I never slept with Young Will or anybody else."

"Bitch, please. You want me to think he was just throwing gifts at you and picking you for his videos for nothing?"

"We are friends."

I roll my eyes and pull my phone out of my pocket. My initial instinct is to go clean off on her, but I don't want the show to revolve around me getting into arguments and fights. I will go to the source of the drama and nip it in the bud. I video dial Young Will, hoping he will vouch for me and my honor. Crazy, I haven't done a music video in over two years. Will and I are still cool though and I am confident—well, I'm hoping—he will answer my call.

Frustrated, I stand in the parking lot waiting for him to answer.

"Yo Billi," he finally picks up the phone and I smile. He looks high as hell and I am glad he wasn't smoking when he answered. I am pretty sure the camera can't see my phone screen but you can never be sure.

"Hey, Will, how you been, yo? It's been a while. Sorry to just pop up on ya' like this."

"Nah, it's cool. I been meaning to call you and congratulate you on the engagement. Hope that dude knows how lucky he is."

"Thanks and yeah, I think he does. I called you because I need a favor. I don't know if you heard, but I'm filming a reality TV show, *Sports Wives*."

"Ah yeah, that's cool. What's up? What you need?" I take a deep breath before making my request. I know how some people, especially famous people, can be when put on the spot.

"That is not Young Will. Bitch, quit fronting," I can hear Traci rapping in the background.

"Who the fuck is that?" Will hears Traci too.

"Some chick that has basically called me a hoe on camera. I need you to—"

"Turn me towards the camera," Will demands. I can tell he is pissed and I smirk a little. Not only have I never slept with him, but he made sure that the other rappers from other videos I was in didn't mess with me either.

"Okay." I turn my phone around towards the camera, making sure that Traci sees Will's face on my screen. I can tell she is shocked and annoyed.

"Yo, Angel Jimenez-Jones and I have never been romantically involved. Not from a lack of trying, but because she is a real good woman. A respectable chick. So any lame ass motherfucka' out there saying otherwise is a got damn lie. This is a PSA from Young Willie, baby," Will finishes and I feel relieved.

"Thank you so much Will," I say gratefully as I turn the phone back towards me and smile at him.

"Was that cool?"

"Yes, definitely."

"A'ight, I'm heading to the studio. Let me know if you need anything else. Hey, and make sure I get my invite to the wedding. I know you gon' have some fine ass bridesmaids."

"Okay," I laugh before hanging up.

"Whatever," Traci says as she walks away, pissed that I burst her bubble.

"Wow, Angel that was cool as hell. I didn't know you and Young Will were that close. Do you think he will be a guest on the show?" Evan asks.

I can see his eyes glowing just thinking about the ratings the show will get if Will makes an appearance. I shrug my shoulders like I don't know, but there is no way I am going to use my friendship with him just to get viewers to tune in. I respect Will and our friendship.

"Okay, well I think you should do a quick testimonial about what happened."

After I film my testimonial, I don't wait to ask Evan if he is done filming for today. I am sure they have more than enough from me and I have other business to tend to. I dial the number Alejandro gave me to contact him. I take a deep breath and wait for him to answer. *God, please let this work out.*

"Bueno?" Alejandro answers.

"Hola, Alejandro. Como estas?"

"I am good, Angel. I will be better once you tell me

where your mother is with my stuff."

"I have it. I don't know what she was thinking and why she did what she did. I just want to get you your money and stuff back."

"Good. Where is Maria, Angel?"

"She told me you don't want her anymore, so I don't think it really matters. Please just tell me how and when I can get you the stuff."

"I will be in Miami soon. You will meet me then. Angel, I expect to get everything she took back. And as for Maria—"

"Look, let's just call it an amicable divorce. I know it won't be legal, but I am sure you are done with her. Por favor, Alejandro. I just want to have my mother back in my life. It's been such a long time. Don't take her from me again."

"Alright, Angel. But do not trust Maria. She is not who you think she is." Alejandro hangs up and I sigh with relief.

That went exceptionally well but I don't believe him; not about my mother anyway. I think he will still try to find her eventually.

Alejandro's words stick in my head as I drive home. "Do not trust Maria." I wonder what he means. Probably some mind game he is playing with me. I just can't wait until this is all over. Now I have to figure out how to make a trip to Miami without Daniel. God, will the drama ever end? I feel doomed to hustle for the rest of my life.

My phone starts vibrating in my lap and I about jump out of my skin. What if it is Alejandro again? I am tempted to not answer. I turn it over and see it is Beau and feel a sense of relief. I need to talk to someone about what is going on and I am glad that it is her.

"What is wrong with you?" Beau yells as soon as I

answer. Oh God, this is not going to be a good conversation. Did GG slip and tell her I quit school before I got a chance to? I don't have time to listen to her fuss at me about my life choices.

"Look, Beau, I am grown and old enough to make my own decisions."

"So you decided to do a reality TV show and bring up some past drama I had with Skylar? Real smart, Angel."

"What? Wait. Who told you? I mean I was going tell you about the show. I've just been so busy. And I didn't bring up that stuff with Skylar. She called you a home wrecking hoe and I was trying to defend you."

"When I walked out of my office today I was bombarded with flashing cameras and questions about why I stole Real from Skylar and the fight we had years ago. You know I tried to put all the foolishness behind me and be happy with my family. Why are you doing a reality TV show anyway? What about school?"

"I dropped out and look, Beau, before you start fussing at me about that too, I figured out what I really want to do with my life. I want to be an actress."

"Are you serious? What is up with you? Look, I can't tell you what to do but at least think about your family. I don't want to hash up old stuff. Keep me, my family, and my business out of your foolishness." Beau hangs up before I have a chance to respond.

So far it seems like this show is causing more harm than good. I pick up the phone to call Kylie; someone I know will just listen and be there for me without criticizing and judging me. My phone starts vibrating before I can dial her number and it's her. Man, we must have some type of psychic connection because I need my bestie right now. With so much drama in the ATL I need a drink and a

94

sympathetic ear.

TESTIMONIAL

"Wow, that was crazy with that Traci chick, huh? How do you feel about her calling you a hoe?" Evan asks, egging me on to elaborate on what just happened.

"Look, I don't knock anybody for how they make their money and I don't regret doing music videos. But I am not about to let somebody come out slandering my name. Yeah, Traci was and may still be a video hoe, a chick that does whatever to get in videos, and so be it. What you do need to know, though, is that not all women are like that. There are some girls out there that get parts the honest way. The money I made doing those videos paid my way through college and I am sure there are much worse ways I could have gotten paid," I say, shaking my head.

"I have always strived to do my best at whatever I do. That meant being the top video vixen and having a 4.0 GPA when I went to college. And now that I want to act, I am going to do my best at that too."

9
Shady Business

Kylie

Contemplating my next move and what I should pray, I stand before a statue of the blessed Virgin Mary. She's wearing a blue robe looking down on me with her arms stretched out, ready to take my prayers and lift them up to God. I don't worship her, but I do recognize her importance as the mother of God and her ability to intercede with her son.

I strum my fingers on the mahogany wood table laden with candles. I light a candle and say a prayer for Brian. I have him on my side and I need him to convince Daddy to let me help run the family business. I light another candle and say a prayer for my unborn child that I'm carrying. My period was late and I took a pregnancy test this morning to confirm my overwhelming joy. I light one more candle and say a prayer for Angel. I don't know what's going on with her, but my intuition tells me something major is going on in her life and the least I can do for her is to send up a prayer to help her get through it.

I go to a pew and kneel down with my rosary beads in my hand. I need to say a prayer and ask for forgiveness for what I'm about to do.

"Our Father, who is in heaven, Holy is your name. Your kingdom come. Your will be done, on earth as it is in Heaven. Give us this day our daily bread, and forgive us our sins…"

I feel a shoulder rub against mine. I look up from my prayer and see Blake kneeling beside me with rosary beads hanging around his neck like a piece of jewelry. Infuriated,

I snatch the beads from around his neck.

"You sacrilegious piece of shit. This is not a necklace," I say, holding up the beads. Wearing rosary beads is the ultimate disrespect. I may not be the best Catholic in the world, but I try not to be blasphemous when I can.

"Dude, you just cussed in church. Wouldn't it be more sacrilegious to rip them like that?" Blake asks, gesturing to the broken rosary beads in my hand.

I grimace at him. To me the bigger offense is his wearing the rosary than the words I used to right his wrong.

"I was trying to look inco...inconspic...inconspicuous."

"We need to talk business, but not in here. Bring yo' inconspicuous ass on."

Some things shouldn't be done in the sanctuary. I get up and go to the vestibule, and am glad the church's lobby is empty so Blake and I can talk business. Blake follows my lead. Before I can turn around to face him, he begins talking.

"Look, I'm not sure if this is the right thing to do?" Blake complains.

"I'm not going to let you back out on me. You're doing this," I say sternly. "What, don't tell me you actually love Skylar?"

Blake scoffs. "Of course not, but I don't want to come off as a jerk. Besides, if I break up with her I'm no longer relevant to the show."

"Tell me why you are on the show in the first place."

"To get endorsements."

"And what am I offering you?" I ask frustrated.

"An endorsement with Rose and Company for a sports vitamin."

"So you're getting exactly what you want. I already

leaked the pictures to the blogs. All you have to do is talk the other guys into driving down to Miami to surprise us ladies and then you drop the bomb. Pretend like you just saw the pictures on the blogs and use that as an excuse to break up with her. Just make sure it's all on camera. She will look like the slut that she is and you will look like a heartbroken bachelor that's back on the market."

"Well that's the problem," Blake whines and I sigh with exasperation as I wait for him to continue. "Everyone knows you don't have anything to do with your family's company. How do I know I will actually get an endorsement and you're not all talk?"

Without saying another word I pull out the contract for the endorsement out of my purse and slam it against his chest.

"Talk to this then."

I convinced Brian to back me on the contract after I showed him that I enrolled in some business college courses and presented a marketing plan for our subsidiary company to him. He was so ecstatic that I am finally becoming more serious about the family business and approved my marketing plan, including Blake's endorsement. The only trick is to get our parents to trust me with it. I don't care if I have to start out as the mail girl; I'm willing to do what it takes to earn that trust back.

A giddy expression comes across Blake's face.

"Are you serious? Is this the contract for my endorsement?"

I nod my head and say in a tone that brokers no argument, "Like I said, you're not backing out of this deal. Got it? I have way too much riding on this."

Blake nods his head with excitement.

"Go over it with your attorney and have him forward

me a signed copy."

I walk out of the church hoping I don't get struck by lightning for using Blake to set Skylar up, but like my daddy always says, "owe no man nothing but to love him." After what Skylar did to me, I definitely owe her and I always pay my debts.

I go home and finish packing for what's supposed to be an all-girls trip in Miami that Angel planned. Logan is at practice and I asked the nanny to take Ethan to watch him. If Ethan sees me packing and walking out the door with luggage, he will fall out crying and my heart can't take watching my little munchkin cry.

I'm startled by banging on the front door. I'm a little scared. Nobody should have gotten past my security gates without me having to buzz them through. I flip the TV on and check the surveillance cameras. It's Mario. I pick up the landline and speak through the intercom.

"How did you get pass the gates?" I snarl.

"A while back Logan gave me a gate key. Why aren't you picking up your phone when I call?"

"Are you serious? You can't be serious. You are fucking my husband and you are questioning me?"

"I was only doing what I needed to do to keep my client happy. He basically told me I had to if I wanted him to sign with me. He means nothing to me. I love you and only you."

I wish he could see me glaring at him through the cameras. Mario continues and his whole disposition changes to attack mode.

"You are the one that forced him on me as a client. It's your fault *we* are in this situation. You wanted him as my client, as a cover up to our love escapades."

"It's my fault now? Do you know how hurtful it is to

100

know that you screwed me and my husband in the same damn day? How much less of woman I feel to know both my husband and my lover are gay?"

"You got to play by the rules to make money, but I'm not gay or nothing. I was on top and he was the one taking the dick. Your husband, the All-American, is gay, not me."

"Leave my property!"

"Baby, please. I don't want to lose you like this. I'll stop. I'm done with Logan, even if that means I'll lose him as a client," Mario begs, but I'm not buying that he is having sex with Logan to keep him as a client, because Logan already signed a five-year contract.

"Don't pretend to love me and have sex with me when you know I'm not what you want. Leave!"

I could use a hit of blow right now, but I can't afford to fall off the wagon, especially not with this baby inside of me.

"Me and our baby don't need you. If I want to live a lie I'll just stay with my husband."

"*Our* baby? You're pregnant?"

"Yeah, bitch. I'm pregnant."

"You're just saying that to get to me."

"Oh yeah? Hold on." I rush to get the pregnancy test I left in the bathroom and dash down the stairs. I jerk the front door open and fling the test in his face.

"That means I'm pregnant!"

"Oh my God. I'm going to be a father! How far along are you?" I can see the dollar signs in his eyes.

"It doesn't matter. We don't need you in our lives. Now for the last time, leave!"

"I'll leave for now, but I'm coming back for mine. You'll take me back or I'll make you pay me in child support checks," Mario threatens as he walks away and gets in his car.

"But you love me, right?"

I slam the door and stomp up the stairs to finish packing. I don't have much time. The party bus that is taking the cast to Miami will be here to pick me up soon. And I sure as heck don't have time to be bothered with Mario's *I have sex with men but I'm not gay* foolishness. I'm done with him. From here on out I'm focusing on making my messed up situations work for me.

While packing I pull my cell phone out. I zip through the internet and find the number I'm looking for. I click on the number and it appears on the keypad of my phone. I hit the call button and wait for someone to pick up.

"Hello, Family Ties DNA, Incorporated. How can I assist you today?" a friendly female voice answers.

"Yes, I need the paternity results of children Israel James and Beaunifide James," I say as I place a pair of red-soled heels in my suitcase.

"I'm sorry, ma'am. I can't give that information out and I certainly can't do it over the phone." The voice is still friendly but stern. I pick up a blouse out of my closet to pack.

"Well why not?" I ask with my hands on my hips.

"Because it's against the law. There are certain privacy laws set in place. Only the father or mother can get those results and a release waiver would have to be signed," the friendly voice advises me.

"Okay. Thank you," I say cheerily and hang up the phone satisfied with the results of my little research.

Just as I'm zipping up my suitcase the gate bell rings. Here we go with the antics. I buzz the party bus through. So far, in just about every scene I've been in I have been arguing with Skylar. It's time to shut her down once and for all and solidify my spot as the queen of the show, which will translate into sales for the Rose empire.

I casually walk outside and hand my suitcase to one of the crewmembers.

"Can you get that for me?" I ask as I get on the bus, making sure everyone aboard can hear me. "I'm in no condition for heavy lifting."

I want there to be speculation that I'm pregnant. Reality TV loves a pregnant chick. I survey the bus. Everyone is here except Angel and I'm instantly disappointed.

"Hello, girls. The Rose is here."

"I wish she would stop saying that. That shit is not catching on," Skylar whispers to Elle sitting at the front of the bus. Elle giggles. I ignore both of them and make my way to Tori and sit next to her at the back.

Tori sighs with relief.

"Thank God you are here," she whispers. "We went to pick Angel up and she was already gone. The producers called her and she told them she wasn't riding on the bus with Skylar because she didn't know what she would do to her after she tried to slander her name. I'm just glad you didn't ride with her and leave me alone with these vultures."

"Hmmm. What is my sister up to?" I accidently wonder out loud. Maybe it was smart of her to avoid Skylar. There's no telling how they will edit all the arguing with her. Skylar is wrong but we could end up looking like the villains if we're not careful.

Skylar nudges Elle. At Skylar's prompting Elle says, "Ugh, she is not your sister. Please explain why you think otherwise."

"She is my sister if I say she is. What's understood

103

doesn't need to be explained."

"Where is she anyway? I still have a bone to pick with her. She must be trying to avoid me," Elle sneers.

Skylar chimes in, "Yep, because she's guilty. I know what I saw."

"Just stop it. You didn't see anything." I cut Skylar with my eyes.

"I saw what I saw," Skylar says, raising her voice louder.

As the tension rises I remember that I don't want to be seen arguing in every scene I appear in on this show. I clap my hands to call attention to the PSA announcement I decide to make. Everyone stares at me like I'm crazy.

"Listen up, ladies. This is a girls' trip to celebrate Angel's and yours truly's life." I make cute pouty lips and point to myself. "And I just want to call a truce. I don't want to fight or argue with anybody on this bus, including you, Skylar. I just want to have a good time...at least until this trip is over."

Everyone agrees to the truce. I mean, you would look like a real jerk to want to carry on the shenanigans after that speech, but there still isn't unity. Skylar and her minions stay in their corner and chat amongst themselves while Tori and I stay in our corner of the bus for the entire road trip. When we get close to Miami, I feel the bus come to a stop. Shannon and Evan climb on.

"Ladies, we are just outside of Miami and we haven't gotten one good shot that we can use," Shannon admonishes us.

Evan chimes in. "You all need to loosen up and have more fun. There are several bottles of champagne on the bus. Drink up."

"Where? You should've told me. I'm down to clown!"

Tori exclaims. Evan points to a pull out compartment on the bus.

"Everyone should have a drink in their hands," Shannon advises before she and Evan exit the bus.

Tori is the first one to pop the cork on one of the bottles and start pouring everyone a glass. Tori tries to hand me a glass and I refuse to take it. She shrugs her shoulder and downs the glass she tried to give me. She picks up another bottle and starts shaking it vigorously as she dances. Then she puts the bottle between her legs and pretends like she is riding it like a horse. She pops the cork on the bottle and it goes flying through the bus landing on the floor next to Jordyn's feet.

Bubbly is overflowing out the bottle and like the true drunk that she is, Tori takes the bottle to the head, gulping it down to the last drop. Tori starts twerking on the pole and I clap my hands to the beat, laughing.

"Get it, girl!" I encourage Tori. "Can't nobody work that pole like you."

"Except for you," Skylar sneers. "I'm surprised you are not guzzling bottles like your porn star friend."

I ignore the jab to Tori. I'm not trying to fight her battle, but this is the perfect time to reveal my big news.

"If you must know, I'm not drinking because I'm pregnant."

Jordyn gasps with delight and Skylar mugs her.

"Oh my gosh. I'm so happy for you," Tori slurs, still twerking on the pole.

"Get the fuck out here. You are not pregnant. I saw you drinking at the gala," Skylar points out.

"I did have a drink. I wasn't aware that I was pregnant at the time," I admit.

"Hoes popping babies like they pop bottles," Skylar

says, smugly. She has insulted me for the last time.

"You would know if you hadn't had so many abortions," I say, forgetting our truce. I dug up some dirt on her to use as ammunition just in case she started with me again. If I'm going to end up arguing with her again on camera at least I can make her look worse than me.

"Don't abort, support," Tori slurs, sliding down the pole.

"Fuck you. I only had one abortion, bitch. At least I'm willing to 'fess up to my mistakes. Just because you're married doesn't erase all your hoe-ness. It was all over the blogs how you used to hoe around and snort cocaine. You are the sleaziest person on this bus," Skylar fires her venom at me.

"Hey, hey. You can't talk to my friend like that," Tori says before falling to the floor as the bus comes to another stop. I glance out the window and see a large granite fountain with the words Eau Fontaine Miami scrawled across it and palm trees waving in the wind.

Beyond pissed, I make my way to the door. I can hear Skylar still taunting me about my past. I jiggle the door handle and the door refuses to open. I turn around and face Skylar and I snap.

"The magic words are 'used to.' You talking about some stuff I did when I was 16. Bitch, you about 48 doing the most. You old enough to be someone's grandma with your saggy titties. Get your titties out your socks and shut the fuck up talking to me."

"I'm not 48, bitch!" Skylar jumps out of her seat and runs towards me full force. Both Elle and Jordyn hold her back.

While Skylar struggles to get loose, Jordyn tries to talk some sense to her.

"Skylar, stop it. Stop it. She's not worth it. She's pregnant. You can't fight a pregnant lady," Jordan states.

I push the door, but it still won't open.

"That slut ain't pregnant!" Skylar reaches her arm out and pops me on top of my head with her purse.

The door opens and I stumble off the bus. I'm not hurt, but I am pissed and embarrassed. Cameras are in my face. In that moment I decide I am going to make this humiliation of getting hit on national TV work for me. I let the tears roll from my eyes.

"I can't believe she hit me," I cry for the cameras. "I hope my baby is okay."

TESTIMONIAL

"Everyone has a history and I'm no different. The things that I did in the past I did as a child, but Skylar is a grown woman and she attacked a pregnant person. No one deserves that. I use my words to fight my battles and not physical violence. Only evil bullies attack pregnant women. The incident is quite sad, especially given that I stated from the beginning that all I wanted to do was get along with everyone," I confess to the camera.

Shannon tries to engage me more, but I have said what I need the public to know about the situation. I get up and as I'm walking out Shannon grabs my arm to stop me.

"Shannon, I don't think you want to do that," I snarl, glancing at her hand gripping my arm. "You and this entire production company will be lucky if I don't sue you. I was attacked while pregnant and your security was nowhere to be found. If it wasn't for your negligence none of this would have happened. Better yet was it negligence or was it intentional? Why didn't that door open? I tried to open it several times and I know you could see me on the cameras

107

trying to get off the bus."

Shannon goes quiet.

"You know if I was to find out that somehow you prevented me from getting off that bus I will file a criminal complaint…that has to be false imprisonment or something."

Shannon lets go of my arm. "I'm sorry. How can we make it up to you?"

I hold my smile inside.

"I want to be an executive producer and have final editing say over every scene that I'm filmed in."

"Done," Shannon says with no hesitation.

"Good. Then we are done here."

Donisha Derice & Jai Darlene

10
Exit Stage Left

Angel

Kylie's and my birthday is the perfect excuse for a girls' weekend in Miami and a good cover for delivering the money and drugs to Alejandro.

"I'll be back before my actual birthday, babe." I look at Daniel as he makes a puppy dog face. I poke my lip out like I am pouting. "It's just the weekend. I only turn 25 once and Kylie and I want to do it big."

I sit on Daniel's lap and wrap my legs around him. I am lying to Daniel. I'd much rather be home with him, but I don't have a choice. My birthday and Alejandro's arrival in the states coinciding must be destiny and I am optimistic everything is going to work out and I will be done with this drama in less than 24 hours.

"Why are you driving by yourself instead of doing the party bus with the girls?"

"Skylar," I partially lie.

I am really driving so that I have a chance to book the second room and hide the stash, but I don't want to be around that trick either. Skylar's sneaky ass saw me with Elle's fiancé the night of the gala and couldn't wait to run back to Elle and let her know that I am a slut having an affair with her man. Add that to the fact that the tabloids ran a picture of my mom running up the stairs of the house and claim Daniel is cheating on me. I know Elle can't wait to confront me and has Skylar egging her on. I don't have time to deal with that bull right now. I know if the real nature of my relationship with Isaque came out my life would be ruined. I have a plan, though. I am going to do what I know best; slick talk and hustle myself out of the crazy situation with Elle and Isaque.

"Don't pack ya' boxing gloves," Daniel laughs, bringing me out of my thoughts.

"Funny."

"But for real, are you going to be okay being around her?"

"Yep, as long as it's not for long periods of time or in confined spaces."

"Funny."

"Look, my GG taught me how to act in public. I promise you I will not embarrass you. I am going to keep my cool."

Skylar is the least of my problems. Handling business with Alejandro is all that has been on my mind and I can't enjoy life—not even my birthday—until this is done.

"I am going to say bye to my mom." I pull Daniel in and kiss him like I will never see him again.

I hold on to him like that, too. In all the dirt I have done I have never been so scared in my life. I really don't know what I am walking into or if I will walk out alive. I have noticed my prayers to God have been very grim lately. Every conversation I have with GG revolves around me asking her to pray for me. I know she can sense something is wrong. I just want to survive this; give Alejandro his stuff, and walk out of his life forever.

"Angel, what is going on with you?" Daniel finally pulls away from my embrace.

"I just hope you know how much I love you."

I feel a single tear run down my face as I swallow my cry.

"Of course I do. Angel—"

"That's all I need to know," I say, cutting Daniel off

111

before he can say anything else.

"Angel." I hear him calling out to me as I walk upstairs. I can't bear to look him in his eyes and tell him another lie; not today.

"Mamá, abre la puerta," I say, knocking on her door. She has been very quiet and nervous acting the last few days leading up to my trip. She has stayed closed up in the room and I have been giving her space.

"I know you are worried, but it is going to be okay," I say to her through the door.

I don't know why she is ignoring me. No, I know exactly why. As much as I have tried to talk reason into her she still wants to meet with Alejandro.

"Mamá,!" I throw the door open, tired of her ignoring me. Her room is empty like no one had ever stayed in it. I look across the hall into the bathroom and the door is wide open and empty. I run into my bedroom in a frantic panic to check my bag.

I am beyond fed up with her. She pops back into my life out of nowhere with baggage, literally—baggage full of stolen drugs and money. The money and drugs is still all there. I feel around my bag for my gun, a pearl handle .22, and grip the handle tight. I take a deep breath and think about all the times my sister took me to the gun range.

"Focus and aim." I remember Bella instructing me as I held her purple pistol she named Greta. "You never know, Angel, us hustlers, including Daddy, have done some dirty shit. We have to stay protected."

Bella and I used to go to the shooting range twice a week until I got it right. I wonder what ever happened to that gun. Bella used to have it on her at all times then it just disappeared. Anyway, I hope I don't have to use my gun tonight, but I will kill Alejandro if I need to. I zip up my bags and go downstairs.

"Have you seen my mom?"

"No, I thought she was in her room."

"Nope. Maybe she's in the garden. Hey, I gotta go. I can't wait to see Kylie. We're going to get chocolate wasted," I giggle and head out the door.

* * * * *

I check into the room I reserved for the meeting, which is in the same hotel the girls and I are staying at. I made sure to book the room under an alias, Kalisha Warren. I rock a black and blonde wig with bangs and a tight little red dress and some thigh-high black boots. I am going for a stripper/escort look.

"We don't usually accept cash," the receptionist says, looking at the stack of bills I place on the counter.

"I reserved the room online with my card, but I lost it and need to pay cash," I reason, smacking the gum in my mouth hard, trying to seem as ghetto and nonchalant as possible. I used a prepaid card to do the reservation so there is no bank account associated with the card. This is a pretty luxurious hotel and I don't know if they would accept the card for full payment.

"Okay, well let me look up your information. He looks down at his computer. "I found your information. If you let me see your card I can just—"

"Look, honey, this is $1,500. More than enough for a one-night stay, a deposit, and a gracious tip for all of your help." I tap the money and smile as I look down at his name tag, which reads 'Leon.'

"Of course, Ms. Warren. I will get you taken care of right now." Leon types up some more information and hands me two room keys.

"Thanks, Leon."

I give a flirtatious smile and switch away.

I hurry to the room and stash the money and drugs under the bathroom sink. I snatch off the tacky wig and throw it on the sink. My curly tresses are happy to be free as I comb through them with my hands. I check my watch. The girls should be here soon. I have to get into happy birthday party mode, at least for now. The room is on the sixth floor, a single bed. I don't need anything fancy for this mission. My regular room is a suite with a king-sized bed, mini bar, and Jacuzzi. I am looking forward to actually being able to enjoy this weekend once this business with Alejandro is finished. I put on a two-piece bathing suit, throw a wrap around my butt and slide into a pair of Gucci sandals. With the hooker attire in the bag I am ready to head to the suite and wait for Kylie.

"Bueno?" I answer a restricted call I am sure is Alejandro.

"Listo, mija?" Him calling me daughter irritates me.

"Si, claro," I answer him coldly. God, I cannot wait to be done with him. I am getting goose bumps and my stomach starts to turn knowing within the next couple of hours I will be alone in a room with this man. I let him know the room number and that I am leaving the key under a flower vase full of pink roses in the lobby.

"Muy bien. Angel, even though the circumstances are less than ideal I look forward to seeing you."

I hang up the phone without responding to him. What does he mean he looks forwards to seeing me? Yeah right. I toss his words around my head, wondering what his real motive was for saying that. I place my gun under the wig. The flat screen TV on the wall is close to the door. I turn it on and tune into a Western channel. I place the volume up as far as it goes and step out the door. *Bang, bang, bang.* I can hear the TV loud and clear from the hall. I walk away from the door, counting my steps as a housekeeper exits another room.

"Whew, someone's TV is loud," I say to the housekeeper.

"No, I think its fine. A lot of people have noises coming out of their rooms." She giggles and nods her head towards a room where there is moaning and groaning. I don't know if that is the TV or real live action, but as loud as the TV is in my room I can still hear the noise.

"What about their neighbors?" I scrunch up my face looking curious. I'm trying to get information out of her without looking too obvious. I can tell she has no idea that the loud TV is in my room.

"The two rooms beside it aren't occupied right now." She smiles and disappears into another room.

My senses are heightened and I am aware of everything around. The hallway is empty now. I notice a 'do not disturb' sign on the room across the hall where the moaning is coming from. Three elevators are approximately 32 steps from my door. It takes the elevator about 45 seconds to get to me. A gay couple hops off before I get on. They are a pair of tall blonde-haired buff guys holding hands and whispering in each other's ears. I see them go into a room about four doors down from mine. I also notice an exit sign for the stairs to the left of my door.

Once in my suite, I immediately head to the mini bar. I need like two, three drinks, but I have to keep my wits about myself so I settle for one. I have a glass of vodka mixed with Red Bull and head down to the pool. The sun is long past set but it is still over 80 degrees out. As I turn right towards the pool, I remember I have to place the key under the vase. I quickly slide it under the vase and walk towards the pool again.

"Angel," I hear Tori slur my name. Sounds like somebody is already turnt up.

"Hey, ladies." I turn around smiling to see that I am the only one smiling. Dang, what has happened already? I see Skylar mugging me as she grabs Elle's hand and pulls her toward the elevator. Jordyn follows closely behind them. I look over at Kylie who looks distraught and upset.

"What's wrong?"

"Did you know she is pregnant?" Tori looks at me blurry-eyed. Man, she is so gone.

"What?" I look over at Kylie who still hasn't spoken. How does Tori know that my sister is pregnant before I do?

"Hey ladies, we need y'all poolside in 15 so we can shoot."

Shannon walks by smiling. I have come to the conclusion that I strongly dislike producers. Since the beginning of this show all they have done is stir up gossip and drama.

"Okay." Kylie frowns.

I hold Kylie back from getting on the elevator with Tori and Shannon, who are going to drop their luggage off.

"What happened on the bus?"

Kylie bites her lip before speaking. She tells me all the bull that went down on the ride here. I feel bad for not being there with her.

"Forget them miserable chicks. It's our birthday weekend and I just got the best gift ever. I'm gon' be an auntie again. I just know it's going to be a girl. Little Rose." I rub her belly as the elevator doors open. "I'll go with you."

"It's okay. Go ahead to the pool and have a drink for

me—something strong. I'll be right back."

"Don't leave me alone with them hoes too long," I say, smiling as Kylie hops on the elevator.

I make my way over to the bar and make myself comfortable.

"Naked Sunset is a specialty drink. It's fruity and delicious," the overzealous bartender says, smiling at me.

"Okay, but give me a double shot of whatever alcohol is going in there. Something white, right?" I wink and the bartender nods. I'd already been sipping on vodka, so I can't switch over to dark. I sit in a seat next to the pool sipping my drink and waiting for everyone else.

"Ew, what's that?" Tori grabs my glass out of my hand and turns it up to take a sip.

"Uhhh Tori, I wouldn't drink after her if I were you." Jordyn smirks. This chick don't even know me.

"Everything you've heard about me came from the mouth of Skylar's hoe ass. That's whose lips you shouldn't be trusting." I roll my eyes.

"Please, bitch. I'm as real as they come." Skylar, Elle, and Jordyn clink their glasses together laughing.

"Yeah, so real that you switched some kids' DNA results just to try to keep a man. Yeah you're real; real scandalous!" Kylie yells with disgust.

"Kylie!" I turn towards her, eyes bucked in shock. I can't believe she said that. If the producers and media find out it's Beau they are going to have a field day and Beau is going to be so pissed at me for putting her business out in the street, even if it wasn't me who said it.

"Bitch, I am going to kill you!" Sklyar drops her glass and starts running towards Kylie. I uncross my legs and stick a foot out as she runs by. Skylar trips on it and falls into a pool seat right in front of Kylie.

117

"Ladies, ladies, ladies!" I hear a bunch of male voices yelling. I assume it's the show security. I don't bother to look back at the voices. I pick up my glass and it sip with a sly smirk on my face. If only she'd hit the ground.

"I swear Kylie, if you weren't pregnant I'd whoop your ass!" Skylar screams.

"What the hell is she talking about, Kylie?" a familiar voice asks. It sounds like Logan.

I turn around and see all the guys—Logan, Daniel, Isaque, Blake, and Antonio—standing behind us. Daniel hunches his shoulders smiling.

"We wanted to surprise y'all. Surprise!"

He leans down and gives me a kiss on the forehead.

"Oh." I smile nervously.

I check my watch and see that I am supposed to meet with Alejandro in less than an hour. How am I supposed to pull this off with Daniel right here smiling in my face? I start contemplating reasons to excuse myself without Daniel wanting to go with me.

"What is she talking about DNA results?" I hear the girls trying to question Skylar who is off in a corner trying to explain things to Blake. Kylie and Logan are sitting in another corner, no doubt having a discussion about why he wasn't the first to know his wife is pregnant.

"Angel, what is Kylie talking about? She's your bestie so we know you know." The girls' questions now turn to me.

"Ask your bestie what the deal is. You follow right after her all the time like you know her so well. Shady business. That's your friend Skylar." I smile, shaking my head. I don't like Kylie saying that stuff about DNA on camera for all the producers and soon the world to hear but I am glad that Skylar's treachery has been brought out.

118

"Keep my name out your mouth, bitch!" Skylar starts walking back towards us yelling. She can only be referring to Kylie or me.

"Your way to deflect from all your dirt is to fight. Quit talking all this mess about people and not expect it to happen to you," I check Skylar.

"You aren't perfect, Angel. You been a video hoe and everything else," Skylar shoots back.

"Never been a hoe in video or in real life. Can you say the same, Skylar? Because I have never in my life depended on a man to take care of me or slept with a man in order to be taken care of. How many athletes have you dated and still no ring?" I can see tears welling up in Skylar's eyes. I promised Daniel I wouldn't fight her so I just killed her with my words.

"We need to talk," Blake says, taking Skylar by the arm. I can tell he is pissed. Finding out your girlfriend is a real money hungry gold digging skank must be hard.

"Don't touch me." Skylar pulls away from him and runs towards the elevators.

"I need a drink. What's up? Y'all down?" Logan asks the other husbands. I hadn't noticed that Kylie is gone. I am sure she is tired of all the drama from tonight.

"Babe, you mind?" Daniel asks me.

"No, go ahead."

That will give me the time I need to meet with Alejandro. I sigh in relief; glad I didn't have to make up a lie to tell him.

"By the way, where's your mom?"

"What? She never came back to the house?"

"No, she's here. I saw her when I was on my way to the bar with the guys. I gave her my key to the room. She said she was going to change and meet us poolside."

119

"Oh, okay. Go hang out and I am going to find her so we can hang out too."

I kiss Daniel and hope he doesn't notice how fast I am breathing. What is she doing? What if Alejandro sees her? I panic, looking every which way in the lobby. I don't see Alejandro or any other shady looking Colombian men. The room key is still under the vase. Now to find mama before it's too late. I wonder what is taking the elevators so long as I impatiently wait.

"Hey." I feel a hand on my shoulder.

I turn around and shove the person who grabbed my shoulder without looking to see who it is first.

"Oh my gosh, Evan. I am sorry."

"It's okay. Are you alright?" He keeps his distance from me.

"Yes, I am fine." I give a fake smile and watch as he nervously walks away. Dang it, he made me miss an elevator. I watch it slowly close and press the up button again. I feel strong hands massaging my back. I thought Daniel was going to hang with the guys. His hands do feel good, though. I feel so tense.

"Why so stressed?" an unfamiliar voice with a thick Spanish accent whispers in my ear. I feel his hands move from my shoulders to my back as he pushes me onto the elevator. The door closes before I can turn around. It's time.

Donisha Derice & Jai Darlene

11
Double Cross

Kylie

I calmly tiptoe out of all the chaos that I caused by the pool and get on the elevator. Angel looked pissed that I even brought up the DNA results and all the other girls seemed to have questions that I was not about to answer on camera. I was intentionally as vague as possible. I didn't say Beau or Real's names so even if people are able to figure out I was referring to them it will all be speculation and rumors. There's no way anyone can get concrete proof of the DNA testing; I checked. However, I know Beau is a very private person and she will be pissed all the same.

Revealing on camera how scandalous Skylar is was not an accident either. To me, the benefit of humiliating Skylar on national TV outweighs Beau's privacy concerns. Besides, Beau didn't do anything wrong in the situation. Skylar was the one so caught up in keeping the penis that was funding her lifestyle that she had no regard for disrupting those children's lives and trying to tear them away from their father. I had to bring Skylar down a notch. Consider me a vigilante of sorts, taking down the bad guys that hurt me and my family one by one, starting with Skylar. The next person is Logan and I'm heading to my room for a phone conference with my attorney to take care of that right now.

I can't take Logan down the same way that I'm doing with Skylar. I have to be more discreet about it. And I definitely can't divorce him. Divorce is not an option, after watching how upset my parents were with my brother for publically embarrassing the family by filing for divorce from Bella. It was all over the news and celebrity gossip blogs and my parents were livid. They didn't even see it coming and they kept yelling at Brian that we are Catholics and Catholics don't get divorced; we work through our problems. Our parents beat it through our heads that getting a divorce is an indication of bad decision-making and people might distrust our ability to properly run our company. Besides, if I was to divorce Logan, I know without a doubt that it would get nasty and he would drag me, all my secrets, and my family's name through the mud. But I don't need a divorce to get Logan to act right. I have other plans for him.

I swipe my keycard and my door unlocks. I hear sobbing and turn my head to see Skylar running towards her room next door with a face full of tears. She is crying so hard that she is oblivious to me standing in the hallway.

Before she can get in her room I yell out to her, "Do you seriously not know who I am?"

"You're the slut that I'm going to fuck up if you keep messing with me. How dare you tell everyone about the DNA results?"

I smirk. She deserved it. I'm tired of being everyone's floor mat. Besides, I'm just getting started.

"There are no cameras here. No need to front."

I walk over to Skylar with no fear. I know she's not going to attack me unless it's going to be aired on TV. Her fighting with me and Angel is the only thing making her relevant on the show and I'm sure it's only worth her while to get it caught on camera.

"You sure you want to get up in my face like that? There's no security here to protect you."

"You're not going to touch me. I know all of your dirty little secrets. I know that you spent some time in jail for check fraud. I know that you snort cocaine. We used to have the same dealer. I also know that you attacked a defenseless girl and left her for dead and tried to pin it on someone else." Skylar's eyes light up as she connects the dots. "That's right, bitch. It was me. And I'm coming for you."

Skylar laughs in a sinister way.

"You can't come for me. I know your secrets, too. I caught you slipping dudes date rape drugs. You'll go down with me."

"Maybe. But I was under duress when you made me do what I did. You committed assault, battery, obstruction of justice, conspiracy. Shall I go on?"

Skylar remains silent with a frightened look on her face.

"I come from a family worth billions. I have the money to back me up and fight a case and cover it up with the media. But you don't. You are nothing and you have nothing," I continue to bluff.

If the world really knew everything I did, all the money in the world couldn't save me. Skylar looks like I struck a nerve by calling her nothing. She slaps me in my face and I don't flinch. I keep my eyes locked on hers. I've been hit harder.

"You've been warned. Everything bad that happens to you on the trip, know that I'm the one behind it. If you stub your toe on a chair, I placed the chair in your path. If your hair falls out I had the hotel maids put Nair in your shampoo. If your boyfriend breaks up with you it's because I told him to do it. I'm coming for you." I continue to keep my eyes locked on hers, trying to shake her up as much as possible. When Blake dumps her I want her to know it was me and know to never fuck with me or my family again.

"There you are." I hear Evan's voice coming up the hallway. "Look at you two looking like old chums."

I step back from Skylar and smile at Evan. Evan's smile turns upside down.

"Well stop it. We don't think it's in the best interest of the show for you two to be friends."

Both Skylar and I look at Evan like he lost his mind. He clears his throat.

"Everything was just getting juicy when you all ran your separate ways. We want to keep the momentum going." Evan pumps his fist in the air. "We need you all back by the pool to continue filming."

Skylar walks into her room and slams her door.

"Where's Angel?" Evan asks me.

"I saw her near the elevator a little while ago."

I shrug my shoulders and walk towards the elevators. So much for my phone conference with my attorney.

Once I make it to the entrance of the pool area the first thing I see is Tori prancing around then sitting on Logan's lap. The rest of the cast minus Angel and Skylar are staring in disbelief, not sure what to do. I pause before going any further, trying to get my bearings on how to handle this situation. Hell, the other husbands on the show are more of a threat than Tori, but I have to play my cards right and let everything unfold naturally. And naturally any wife would be upset at a woman flirting with her husband, especially a friend.

From where I stand I scream, "Get away from my husband!"

I start to walk over to where they all are sitting with a grimace on my face. Tori looks shocked and jumps up out of Logan's lap.

"I…I…" is all Tori can muster out.

"I always defend you. Always. Whenever someone calls you a slut or man stealer. I just never thought you would do it to me."

"I'm sorry. I just sat down. I didn't think it was a big deal."

"Sitting your half naked body on my husband's lap is a very big deal."

"I didn't think anything of it. I'm sorry."

"You're right. You don't think and you are a sorry excuse for a friend."

I move past Tori and confront Logan.

"Really, Logan? How could you?" I ask with a little tremble in my voice. Tori grabs another drink and tosses it back.

"Bae, she sat down before I had a chance to stop it." He reaches out and gently pulls me towards him. I sit on his lap, remembering we have to play the perfect couple role. "You're the only girl I want sitting in my lap."

The cast exclaims a group 'awww' as we kiss and make up.

"You could have at least pushed her off you," Blake jokes, referring to Tori.

"No. I would never put my hands on a woman. I'm just not that type of guy, you know? It all happened so quickly. I didn't have a chance to do anything."

The smile on my face says I love my husband, but my eyes tell a different story.

Out of the corner of my eye I see Skylar stroll in. I glance over at Blake and raise my eyebrow to indicate that it is show time. She tries to approach Blake with a kiss, but he swerves his head away.

"Whew. Is there a breeze in here? I need a sweater. It's a little nippy out today!" I exclaim.

126

Skylar ignores me and keeps her attention directed to Blake.

"Baby, what's wrong?" she asks.

Blake pulls out his cell phone and pushes a couple of buttons. A cameraman rushes up behind him to get a closer shot.

"This is what's wrong."

He shows Skylar what's on the phone and the cameraman tilts his camera to capture what Blake is showing her. From where I'm sitting I can't see the phone, but I know what's on it. He pulled up a picture on a blog captioned, "In Baller Boo News: Didn't Know You Could Get Prego From Slurping Man Juice." Under the caption are two pictures of Skylar. In the first one she has her mouth wrapped around somebody's man part, sucking it like it's the best popsicle ever. The second one is of her walking out of an abortion clinic.

Skylar's eyes widen and I can see all the colorful expressions she must be feeling flash across her face, beginning with embarrassment and ending with panic.

"Blake, I can explain."

I scoot to the edge of Logan's lap, excited about what's about to happen. I wish I had some popcorn for this show.

"No need to. These pictures explain it all. You played me, got pregnant by someone else, and had an abortion to cover it up," Blake says, shaking his head. "I'm away a lot traveling so you had plenty of opportunity. I know what's up."

"No. No, those are old. Someone dug up some old dirt on me. I swear, I would never." Skylar grabs his arm and he pulls away.

"This is something I can't deal with. Do you know how much I loved you? Maybe…maybe we need some time apart." Blake looks away from Skylar, but she gently turns his face back towards her.

"Please tell me you're not breaking up with me. Are you breaking up with me?" Skylar is in full begging mode and I'm loving it.

In a gentle voice Blake says, "Yes, Skylar, I am." *Yes, honey. Yes!*

A look of agony crosses Skylar's face because she just lost another paycheck.

"You came all the way down here just to break up with me?" she asks, sounding frustrated and hurt.

"I came to surprise you and when I got here someone sent me that blog article. Then I hear something about you ruining children's lives and switching DNA tests. I just can't trust you anymore. I love you but it's over."

Blake kisses her on the forehead with finality and walks away.

It's as if I can hear the pieces of Skylar's heart breaking and the corners of my mouth are touching my ears. My debt is paid. She takes off running behind him, crying and screaming,

"You can't do this to me! How dare you!"

She catches up to him and starts hitting him on the chest repeatedly before security steps in and drags her away. Everyone watches on with expressions of shock on their faces—except for me.

SPLISH.

Water splashes all over me. I look over at the pool and see Tori flapping her arms in the water. I panic, jumping up and pointing.

"Someone save her! She's drowning."

Logan dives in to rescue her, shoes and all. Tori is still flapping her arms, trying to keep above water, and

128

accidently hits him in the face as he tries to grab her waist. He pulls her to safety on the side of the pool.

As Logan is lifting Tori to the ledge she wraps her arms around him and kisses him on the lips.

"Dammmmmmn," Antonio, Jordyn's husband, and Isaque say at the same time.

"Thank you so much for saving me," Tori's says after their lips part.

All eyes turn to me to catch my reaction, but I'm too baffled by what just happened.

"If I knew you were going to do that I would have let you drown," I hiss at Tori. "Logan, get out of that water and let's go. Now!"

I storm off towards the elevator and soon hear Tori running up behind me.

"No. Kylie, wait. It's not like that. I was just thank—" Tori pleads her case before I hear her stumble to the ground. I don't turn around to check if she's okay. I just yell at Logan that he better hurry up.

We make it up to our suite and Logan slams the door behind us.

"Who do you think you are talking to me like that?" he screams.

"The same person I've always been."

I throw my arms up and turn around towards him.

"I should—" Logan lifts his hands up to slap me but I duck and dodge towards the door.

"So you're just going to hit your pregnant wife?" I ask, backing closer to the door.

"I swear I want to choke you." Logan lunges towards me. I sidestep and slap him as hard as I can, trying to slap some sense into him. He looks at me angry and shocked. He must be stunned because I never hit him before. I only took the hits.

"That's right. This ends today. You will never ever put your hands on me again."

"And what exactly are you going to do?" Logan steps toward me slowly.

"Call the police and have you arrested. I'll make a public police report that you became violent against me after I caught you with another man. I'll shatter your All-American boy image by showing the world the piece of trash that you really are."

Logan gets in my face. I can feel his warm breath.

"You will never tell on me because I'll tell on you."

"I'm willing to go down with you if that's what it takes to end this. I can't have my children growing up thinking it is okay for daddies to hit their mommies."

"Times have changed. I can come out and be accepted. Look at Michael Sams. Especially in Atlanta. I'll be a hero."

"No one is going to celebrate you. Heroes don't deceive and batter their wives. That's the difference between Michael Sams and you."

He started his professional football career being open and honest. If Logan can't see the difference, I'll be happy to point it out with the media there to catch it all.

Logan paused, contemplating his next words.

"What if I leaked to the media that you tricked me into getting you pregnant? You knew about my situation all along and knew I was on the verge of leaving you so you got pregnant on purpose?"

I laugh hysterically.

"So do you really think people are going to believe that your wife is trying to trap you? We're already married and we don't have a pre-nup. And you call me stupid."

Logan moves swiftly and before I realize what is happening he pins me against the door by my neck.

"When did you become such a cold-hearted bitch? Why didn't you tell me you were pregnant first? What are you up to?"

"I'm pregnant, because *you* wanted me to be pregnant. You wanted this; not me. Until recently, you hadn't touched me since Ethan was born." A tear rolls down my eye. "When I was pregnant with Ethan, it was the only time I truly felt loved by you. Don't question my heart when you are the one responsible for breaking it."

I push Logan's hand away from my neck and walk out, slamming the door.

TESTIMONIAL

"This has been *the* worst birthday celebration ever! I have been hit in the head, attacked by a vicious aging mule, and betrayed by my so-called friend all in less than 24 hours," I fume.

Shannon smiles. "So is it true what you said about Skylar?"

"Do I look like TMZ to you? I'm not in the business of selling stories, so I have nothing to gain by lying. And I can't blame Blake for breaking up with her. I just feel so bad for him. When you really love someone and you find out how manipulative and scandalous they are it's heart-breaking. But the best thing he can do is move on. She's only going to continue to hurt his heart and his pockets."

Shannon raises her eyebrow. "What do you mean by hurt his pockets?"

"Well you didn't hear it from me, but I know for a fact that Blake was in negotiations for an endorsement deal and now that those pictures of Skylar leaked..." I point my finger downwards and whistle a falling torpedo sound. Later I will reveal that I gave Blake an endorsement deal and it will seem like I am doing it out of goodwill since Skylar has ruined his life.

"So you mean to tell me Blake's brand is plummeting because of his association with Skylar?" Shannon asks, enthused about the revelation. I twist my lips to the side and look her up and down as if to say *you know it, girl.* "And Tori—"

"Don't mention her name to me. I don't know in what world it's okay to kiss another woman's husband. Not in my world. And I'm not buying the 'I was drunk' excuse either. She crossed the line."

Donisha Derice & Jai Darlene

12
Miami Vice

Angel

I don't get a good look at his face, but I know it's not Alejandro. He has sent one of his henchmen. He is so weak he had to send a goon to deal with me. I feel my heart jumping and sweat forming on my face and neck, making my hair stick to it. The goon's hand grips my arm tightly and I finally turn around.

"No..." I try to blurt out when I see him push the button to go to the suite. Obviously he has been watching me, but not long enough to see me go to the other room first.

"Shut the fuck up." His grip gets tight around my arm. I watch as the elevator passes floor after floor, including the one we should be heading to. I want to tell him but I am too scared to talk.

When the elevator finally opens I don't move.

"It's not in that room. I..." I try explaining again.

"You little dumb bitch, it better be here." He shoves me off the elevator and I am relieved that the hall is empty as I quickly walk towards the suite. Why didn't Alejandro tell him where the room is? I stand at the door waiting for him to pull out the key and realize he is at the wrong room.

"Open it." He shoves me up against the door and I quickly comply. As soon as the door opens I can feel the cold metal of a gun on my back.

"Tony, what are you doing?" I hear my mother screaming. I look up to see her going through my bags. My panties, dresses, and shoes are thrown all over and the bed is disheveled. The room is totally ransacked.

134

"Mamá, qué haces?!" I scream at her confused. She looks sweaty and weird. Her eyes are bucked and glazed over. She is high on something.

"Angel, just tell Tony were the shit is!" she yells, looking right through me. This Tony guy is not with Alejandro. He is with her.

"Oh my God." Alejandro's words about not trusting her replay in my head.

"Where is it?" Tony pushes me. I turn around to face the barrel of the .45 pointed at my head and get my first good look at Tony. He is young—late 20s, early 30s—but looks worn out and stressed. His hair is cut very low to his head and his skin is a deep-tanned caramel. His eyes are bloodshot red and bucked just like Mamá's. He wipes the sweat dripping down his face with his free shaking hand

"Where's Alejandro?" he asks, still pointing the gun at me.

"I...I..." I try to stutter out an answer but my phone rings before I can finish. I know it is Alejandro.

"Answer it," Tony demands, waving his gun.

I take a deep breath. "Hola, Alejandro."

"Estoy aqui."

I am late and he sounds irritated.

"Lo siento. I am on my way." I hang up the phone. I have to get myself out of this or I am dead. If Tony doesn't kill me Alejandro will for thinking I betrayed him and set him up. "The stuff is in another room." I finally get the words out.

"Maria, stay here," Tony commands my mother. I look over at her, feeling betrayed and disgusted. She can't even look me in my eyes.

"Let's go."

Tony snatches me by the arm. He slides his gun into

135

his waistband and we exit the room. I walk down the hall to the elevators and freeze when I see a hotel room door open. God, please don't let it be anyone I know. A Barbie and Ken looking couple walk out and I sigh a little relief, but I know this is far from over. The elevator opens and we all get on. Tony pulls me close to him. I feel sick as his hand touches me, moving my hair from my neck. He leans in and takes a deep inhale, his lips lightly kissing my neck.

"Please stop," I plea through tight lips.

"You are so beautiful and smell so sweet. I bet your pussy tastes sweet too."

He puts his hand under my wrap and starts rubbing my vagina. Ken and Barbie are too busy kissing and flirting to notice what is going on. I am repulsed by his touch and try moving his hand but can't. Tony grabs my vagina tightly and it hurts. "I am going to fuck you," he whispers in my ear.

My legs buckle and I start to slowly slide to the ground. Him violating me never crossed my mind. The elevator opens and I consider running down the hall but then the thought of a bullet exploding into my back stops me.

Once again the hall is empty and it is quiet, all except the loud television coming from my room. I feel a bulge from Tony's pants and know it's not his gun, because he already has it sticking me in my back.

"Open it." Tony forces me into the door and stands off to the side, gun pointed in my direction. I take a deep breath and slowly open the door.

Alejandro stands with a large grin on his face, arms outstretched for a hug.

"Hola, mija." I stare at him with a look of desperation. I want to run into his arms away from Tony. Right now Alejandro is definitely the lesser of the two evils.

Alejandro's face turns to a look of concern when he sees me shaking and not moving.

"Hola, Alejandro." Tony and his gun finally enter the room. Alejandro has no time to grab the pistol I see sticking out from his side.

"Tony."

Tall and regal, Alejandro looks down at Tony who stands about 5'4" to Alejandro's towering six feet. I am left standing in between them and by the mutual looks of hate and disgust, I can tell they know each other well.

"You traitor motherfucking cabron," Alejandro sneers at Tony.

"Whatever, old man. I am going to kill you, fuck her, kill her, take the money and dope, and disappear." Tony gives a sick laugh. "You've gotten too old and weak for this, Jefe. I got that puta dope fiend wife of yours to set you up so easy. Look how easily you let your guard down. She knew your daughter was the key."

Tony laughs again.

She used me. This whole time she was playing me. She knew I would never let her meet Alejandro by herself after she told me how he treated her. Now I feel like it was all lies to get me down here to Miami with the stuff and to get Alejandro alone. She also knew he wouldn't bring his henchmen just to come meet with me.

"Don't touch her!" Alejandro yells. I see something in his eyes—concern and the love of a father. Oh my God. All this time my mother had me thinking this man hates me and wants nothing to do with me, but right now looking in his eyes I feel like it was all lies.

"Like this?" Tony grabs my left breast, squeezing it tightly all while still pointing his gun at Alejandro. He snatches my bikini top off. My body slightly jerks forward.

"Maybe I should tie you up and make you watch me fuck her." He unties my wrap and as I watch it fall to the floor I feel the string on my bikini bottoms loosen and then fall to the floor too.

"I will kill you!" Alejandro growls. But I know there is nothing he can do with a gun pointed right at his head and Tony knows it too. Alejandro turns his head as Tony starts fondling me, defiling my treasure. I feel helpless and sick to my stomach as he rubs his dirty fingers over my clit, stroking it and then inserting his index finger into me.

Tony takes his finger out of me and licks it. "Mmmm, I knew you'd taste sweet. You are so tight. I can't wait to stick my dick inside that tight wet pussy. You feel that?" He grabs my hand and forces me to rub on his dick through his shorts.

"Business first. Go get the shit." He pushes me and my naked body falls into Alejandro's arms. I can't hold it back anymore and begin to sob.

"Shh, shh, mija. Everything is going to be alright." Alejandro tries to console me but I know it is not going to be okay.

"Go!" Tony yells, startling me. I scurry into the bathroom to get the heroin and money.

I glance in the mirror naked and shivering. I almost don't recognize myself. I am Angel Maria Jones. I am stronger than this. I reach under the sink where I taped the money and dope and remember my gun. It should still be under the wig. I feel for it and freeze when I touch the cold metal in my hand. I quickly grab it, knowing the safety is already off.

"Hurry up, bitch!" I hear Tony's agitated voice yell. I can't see him, but through the mirror I see Alejandro staring in his direction. If I wait just another minute or so he will walk closer into my line of view. I know I will only get one chance to kill him so I am going to aim for his head.

I quickly grab the dope and money just as I see Tony walking towards the bathroom with his gun still pointed at Alejandro.

"Did you hear me, puta?" A smile crosses Tony's face when he sees the drugs and money in my hands. But it quickly fades as I drop the stuff, aim, and quickly pull the trigger.

BANG! The sound of the gunshot rings through my ears and I watch Tony fall to the ground with blood leaking from his head. Alejandro leans down and takes the gun from Tony's hand. I focus the gun on Alejandro. I have no idea what he is going to do next. I am in control and plan on keeping it that way.

"Put the gun down, Alejandro. Now!" I scream.

"I am not trying to hurt you, mija."

"Shut up. I didn't ask for any of this. Y'all have ruined my life." The gravity of what has just happened starts to sink in and I am once again crying. I killed a man and there is heroin, $100,000 in drug money, and a drug lord all in this room. When the police bust through the door my life is over.

"Mija, there is so much I need to tell you but right now I need you to put the gun down so I can get this mess cleaned up." Alejandro puts Tony's gun on the bed hoping I will follow suit and put mine down. He bends down and starts picking up my clothes and hands them to me, never looking directly at me like he is ashamed or embarrassed. I grab the clothes out of his hands, my gun still aimed at him.

"I am getting my phone," he announces then turns his back to me and pulls a small flip phone out of his pocket. The television is still on so I can't really make out what he is saying but I do hear the word *limpia*. He has called a cleaner to take care of Tony's body and maybe me too.

"I don't trust you," I tell him, continuing to aim at his head. I have to get out of here before whoever he called gets here.

"Someone will be here in about ten minutes to take care of all of this. Angel, you need to trust me."

"NO!" I scream, staring at Alejandro. *Okay, okay. What am I going to do?* I need to protect myself. I grab Tony's gun from off the bed.

"Take out your gun," I order Alejandro.

I snatch his .45 from him and then gesture for him to have a seat in a chair. I have the .22 aimed at him and the .45 at the door. When whoever Alejandro called comes, I will leave out—naked, gun toting, and all. I am not going to die tonight.

When the knock comes at the door I gesture for Alejandro to answer it.

"Jefe." A tall slender Colombian guy walks in, instantly surprised by the sight of a young naked woman holding two guns. "What have you gotten yourself into?"

He looks at Alejandro and then me, staring at my body.

"Don't look at her. That's my daughter!" Alejandro yells.

"Angel?" The Colombian man quickly turns his eyes from me and focuses on the dead body on the ground. *He knows who I am?* I just stare at him. He doesn't look familiar to me.

"Limpia," Alejandro commands.

"Tony." He finally looks down and mugs Tony's lifeless body

"He and Maria set me up. Angel saved my life." Alejandro gives a proud smile, never looking my way.

"I can fix this, but I need to get him up before the blood seeps into the carpet any more. Jefe, tell your daughter to put the gun away so I can work."

"Get dressed please. Angelita, let me take care of this. I swear to you I have never and will never hurt you," Alejandro pleads with me, not once raising his voice.

"Okay." I place both the guns on the bed and wait for what is next. Alejandro wraps the guns in the blanket and hands it to the cleaner.

"Javier, I am going to walk my daughter to the elevator and then leave. Call me when this is done."

"Si, Jefe, claro." Javier lays Tony's leaking head on the blanket. "Leo is on his way up to help. Hurry and get her out of here."

I quickly throw on my bathing suit, wrap, and shoes and grab my phone. Finally feeling a little composed, I walk out of the room with Alejandro.

"You tried to warn me about her?" I ask as we wait for the elevators.

"Si. Angel, you don't know your mother. I wish you had never trusted her. Maria is only for Maria and will use and run over whoever to get what she wants. I do not have the time to explain everything. Just know everything she has ever told you is a lie. I always knew you were not my daughter but I never forced her to get rid of you. One day I will tell you and you will understand everything."

Alejandro kisses my forehead as the elevator door opens and he gets on. Just like that he is gone and I am left with so many questions.

The elevator heading up finally arrives and I hop on. I want to break down, scream, cry, or hit something but I can't. As soon as I get off the elevator I am greeted by Evan and the camera crew.

141

"Angel, where have you been? Everyone has been looking for you. We needed to do another shoot poolside. Everyone was there except you. Anyway, we still need to shoot your testimonial."

I hear Evan loud and clear but choose to ignore him, not saying a word as I go into the suite. *Sports Wives* is the last thing on my mind. As I expected, Maria is nowhere to be found. The room is empty and all tidied up like she had never torn it up looking for the dope and money she stole from Alejandro.

I start peeling out of my bathing suit and wrap. I want to burn them. I feel some kind of way and just want to take a nice hot shower. I turn the water up as hot as I can handle it and scrub my body until I feel like my skin might peel off. I pay special attention to my treasure and clean it over and over again. When I finally feel clean I turn off the shower and dry off. I wish this had all been just a nightmare, but I know it was not. I will probably have nightmares about what just happened for a very long time. I have to get my mind off of what just happened or I am going to lose it.

I freeze before I can walk out of the bathroom when I hear the suite door open and close. What now? Is Mamá back looking for Tony? Did she and Tony come with other people? Oh my God, what if it's the cleaner coming to finish me off? I look around the room for a weapon. There is nothing. I left the gun with the cleaner to get rid of. How could I have been so stupid? I stand behind the bathroom door waiting for whoever is out there to bust in.

"Angel." I hear Daniel's voice and instantly feel so relieved. I walk out of the bathroom naked, not worrying about wrapping the towel around myself. Daniel's eyes are glued on my naked body. He has never seen me completely naked. He is entranced by my curves and full breasts.

"You are so perfect." Daniel walks up, wrapping his arms around me, caressing my back and butt. I accept his embrace and my body starts to tremble as he lays me on the bed and starts caressing and kissing my breasts and neck. He pauses for a second, waiting for my disproval. I've told him I wanted to wait until our wedding night before we had sex. But I need him. I want him. It feels so good in his arms. This will help me forget.

I feel his stiffness on my inner thigh through his shorts. It's not the first time I have felt his penis against my body, but I have never seen it or come this close to having sex. I watch as he slides out of his shorts and underwear and I catch my first glimpse of his dick. It is long and thick with a slight curve. I brace myself as he slowly pushes my legs apart and I feel the head of his penis gently pressing in. I bite my lip and close my eyes even though I know he is trying to be as gentle a possible. Each stroke he enters deeper into me hurts. I feel a tear run down the side of my face. Daniel kisses my tear and then softly kisses my clinched mouth.

He is deep inside me slowly inching in and out. It hurts and feels good all at the same time.

"Ohhh my…I love you, Angel," Daniel whispers and pants in my ear. I don't say anything. I just continue to lay there, but I can't hold back my moans when he pulls out and starts massaging my vagina with his tongue and lips. I feel my whole body shaking. I have never felt like this before. It's like I don't have control over my own body. I cum over and over again as he continues to nibble and suck on my clit.

"Ahhh…ahhh…ahhh," I moan, unable to utter words. Daniel finally stops eating me out and slides his dick into me again. It hurts a little less than the first time but I still feel every bit of him as he slowly starts taking deep strokes. He pulls both my legs into his arms.

"Ohhh…" I grimace, feeling him further inside of me.

"I'm sorry. I'm sorry," he apologizes, letting my legs down. He was so caught up in the moment he must have forgotten I was a virgin and not ready for all types of positions yet. After a few more strokes Daniel yells out and then collapses on top of me.

"I love you, Angel," Daniel whispers and kisses in my ear as he rolls over to the other side of the bed.

"I love you too," I reply, my voice cracking. I quickly get out of bed to go to the bathroom, noticing the blood-stained sheets. What have I done? I quickly turn on the shower and submerge myself in it again. I sit down under the water sobbing.

"Oh my God. Oh my God."

I feel the enormity of everything that has happened tonight. Life, death, and my most precious asset had all hung in the balance tonight. I will never be the same. I killed a man. I took a life. Flashes of Tony's lifeless body falling to the ground play in my mind. It is all her fault. I hate her I hate her. My mother. She betrayed me. My tears mix with the water and I hope my cries are drowned out by the sound of the shower. I know it's over. I made it, but at what cost? I don't know if I can go back to being the same fun, carefree girl anymore. I feel like within two hours I have aged years and seen so much of life.

"Why me? Why?!" I scream out to God, expecting an answer.

I never asked to be born into this family or into this life.

I quickly get dressed after my second shower and sit on the edge of the bed.

"I thought you wanted to wait until you were married,"

Daniel says, getting my attention.

"What?" I turn, looking at him confused as he is still lying in the bed.

"Sex. You always said you were waiting for marriage."

"Why does it matter? You weren't worried about me waiting 'til I got married a few minutes ago when you were dicking me down whispering I love yous in my ear."

I jump up off the bed as he sits up, trying to lean towards me.

"Why are you getting upset? I was just asking a question. You know—"

"I know if you were so damned concerned with me keeping my virginity you should have been asking questions before you stuck yo' dick all up in me."

"Angel, what is up with this attitude? Did I miss something? We just made love for the first time and now you are upset with me. Is there something you need to tell me?" Daniel looks a mixture of confused, concerned, and frustrated.

"Not now, Daniel. Please."

"If not now, when?"

"Look, I did it. We had sex. Just leave it at that!" I scream.

"I never forced the issue. Angel, if you didn't want to—"

"I'm done with this. I told you not now."

I put on some sandals and pick up my bags.

"What are you doing?" Daniel jumps up and grabs one of the bags from my hands.

"Leaving. I am going to drive back to Atlanta and stay at my condo for a while."

I snatch the bag out of his hand and head to the door.

"What? Why? We are having an argument. Couples

argue. Angel? Angel."

I can hear Daniel calling after me as I walk out the suite and to the elevator. I have to strongly consider if this is really the life for me. As soon as I walk out of the room, Evan's stalking self catches me trying to leave and asks about the testimonial again. I reluctantly comply.

"Angel." I hear Kylie's voice as I try to exit the hotel after finishing my testimonial. Tears are running down her face as she rushes over to me.

"What's wrong?" we both ask one another.

Kylie shakes her head.

"Are you leaving right now? Logan and I got into an argument and I'm ready to go."

"Yeah, me too." Kylie looks at me confused. "I mean yeah, I'm leaving and I got into an argument with Daniel too. Let's go."

During the car ride back, I finally get the chance to speak to my best friend. I give her the blow by blow of the argument with Daniel, leaving out what happened with Alejandro, my mother, and Tony. When I'm done she tells me that she caught Tori flirting with Logan and that she even kissed him. I guess Tori is out of the circle. She can't be trusted. Too bad; I kind of liked her. I'm a little shocked, though. Logan never came off as the type of person to cheat.

"So do you think they are messing around?" I ask, referring to Logan and Tori. "You know Logan is her type; white guy, blonde hair, nice build."

Kylie quickly wipes the tears rolling down her face and looks out the window.

"I don't know. At one point I thought he was cheating with the nanny, but now..." Her voice trails off and she goes silent.

146

I want to ask what she meant. This had to be going on for a long time if she had suspicions of another woman. I'm hurt that she never talked to me about it, but I'm not going to interrogate her about what she's not telling me, because I don't want her to interrogate me about what I'm not telling her.

TESTIMONIAL

"So that was crazy at the pool earlier. Seems like everyone was having issues with each other, huh?" Evan starts to probe.

"No, not really," I answer dryly, rolling my eyes.

"What do you think about what Kylie said about Skylar? If that is true—"

"It's not a matter of whether or not it is true because Kylie wouldn't lie about something like that. So of course it's true."

"But Skylar says it is all lies."

"Would you admit on camera and in front of your man if you had done something so devious, lowdown, and deceitful? DENY, DENY, DENY! Don't expect her to own up to her dirt."

"What about Jordyn and the comment she made about you?"

"Jordyn doesn't know me. She's just trying to stay relevant and I don't have any plans on helping her. Why is she on the show again? Epic casting fail. She is so dull and boring."

"I am sure Jordyn has her own dirt."

"We all have dirt and have done things we regret. Some people are just better at cleaning theirs up."

"So what's your dirt, Angel?"

"Are you serious?" I snatch off the mic and throw it at

Evan who looks scared as hell of me. He should be. I storm out of the room and towards my car.

Donisha Derice & Jai Darlene

13
Villains

Kylie

"Argh!" Logan explodes before he powers his throwing arm through the wall, making it feel like the entire bedroom shakes. Wall plaster crumbles to the floor, leaving a wide hole where he punched it. The framed picture of us in our wedding bliss comes crashing to the floor.

Sitting on the bed I cross my legs and tilt my head.

"Geesh! Stop smashing the wall before you hurt your throwing arm. You have a game coming up and we need to keep up the winning streak. It's great publicity and it ups your star power," I sneer. Logan's violent antics no longer affect me. I have finally gained the upper hand in this relationship.

"Is that all you care about?" he yells, referring to my comment about keeping up appearances.

"Yep, and you are signing these."

I wave some papers in the air. I didn't ask for any of this. I was forced into doing the show and manipulated into a marriage that turned out to be fraudulent. I'm just trying to make the best out of a bad situation.

"I'm not doing it, Kylie! So drop it," Logan demands, shaking his right arm.

I jump up.

"You're signing it!" I scream and throw the papers in Logan's face.

"Like hell I am," he retorts. "I didn't make you sign a pre-nup, so I'm not going to sign a post-nup.'"

"Argh!" It is my turn to grunt in frustration.

"I took you in when your family turned their backs on you and—"

"Don't say that!" I interrupt. "My family didn't turn their backs on me!"

They were just giving me the tough love that I needed by cutting off the financial source I was using to fund my party addictions.

Logan talks over me. "And now that you are about to get your funky trust fund you're trying to cut me out. No. You're probably going to file for divorce the moment I sign. Uh-uh. I'm not doing it."

"I'm not filing for divorce. Did you even read it? It protects us both. It's more of a confidentiality agreement if anything. Both of our secrets are protected."

"No!"

"Listen, this post-nup says you can do what you want. We both can see whoever, as long as they sign confidentiality agreements and we're discreet about it. We keep up public appearances and it lays out how the money will be distributed. I am very generous with how much of my trust fund you get."

Logan looks at me with a look of disgust on his face.

"You? Generous?" I know he wants to hit me, but after I threatened him in Miami he's frightened of what I might do.

"It's a trick. I don't trust you," he adds.

"You're cheating on me and you don't trust me. What have I done that you know of that makes you not trust me?" I pause and wait for a response that I know will never come. "When we got married I loved you. When we took those vows I meant them. Did you love me? Were you even attracted to me?" As I pour out my feelings I mean every word. Logan looks at me exasperated.

151

"Please, I need answers. I'm not judging you. I just need to know why you treated me the way that you did."

Logan looks through me.

"You are just using my situation to go out and be the whore you were when I met you and now you want to leave me out to dry. I guess it's true what they told me about you. You're white trash served on a golden platter."

Logan has insulted me for the last time. I turn towards the door.

In a calm voice I say, "I have to go film. Have your attorney read over the post-nup. Not signing it is not an option."

I walk out the bedroom and gently close the door. I can hear Logan screaming that he is not signing the papers as I walk down the hallway.

I make my way to the garage, hop into the Jag, and drive off. From the car I call Angel to check on her. After she told me she lost her virginity then had a huge argument with Daniel, I've been a little worried about her. She held on to her virginity for 25 years waiting on marriage. It makes no sense that all of a sudden she would give it up without saying those vows. And it seems to me like she was the one to pick an argument with Daniel. I know she's not telling me everything. My feelings would be hurt if I wasn't keeping my own secrets.

"Hello," Angel says, sounding tired.

"Hey, boo. How are you feeling?" I gently ask.

"What's that noise? You have me on speaker?" Angel avoids my question and I roll with it. I get it; she doesn't want to talk about it.

"Yeah, I'm in my car. I'm on my way to film a scene."

"Good luck with that. I won't be filming today. Did I tell you I got the lead role in the movie?"

152

I scream in her ear. I'm so excited for her even though she doesn't sound excited at all. Something is really going on with her, but she won't say what it is. I wish I could give her a hug.

"I can't believe I know a movie star! I know you are going to slay it. Like, oh my gosh!" I say, trying to hype her up about all the wonderful opportunities she has been given.

"And you know this," Angel jokes and we laugh. It feels good. We haven't laughed together since we began filming *Sports Wives*. I try to think of something else to say to keep Angel's spirits up.

"Oooh, girl, I was on BlacLuv.com this morning. You know the hotel we were staying at in Miami? Wellll…" I say, drawing the word out. "It reported rumors of people hearing a gun go off. Some type of shooting or drug deal gone wrong or something like that."

"When?" Angel asks with a little intrigue in her voice. I'm glad my random blog gossip is lifting her spirits.

"While we were filming! Isn't that crazy? The blog did say it was only a rumor and that there is absolutely no proof of any crime other than reports of hearing a gun go off. But you know, there is always some truth to every rumor. And the fact that we happened to be filming there…umph, the tabloids are going to have a field day, especially with all the drama that we filmed."

"Yeah, that's crazy. Oh, hold on. Beau is beeping in. Let me call you back."

As soon as we hang up my hands-free car system starts talking to me.

"You have a call from Brian," the computerized voice alerts me.

"Answer," I sigh.

I really don't want to talk to him. After I leaked that stuff about Skylar to the media, it's been highly publicized that Angel and I are filming a reality TV show. I know he knows about the show and I don't have the energy to face him.

"So you thought I wasn't going to find out?" Brian's voice barks at me.

"It would've been nice if you didn't," I say, sounding defeated.

"Little miss smarty pants, I don't like your attitude. Everything you have been trying to build is going to be ruined because you want to be a Z-list celebrity. What am I supposed to tell Dad?"

"Tell him that Nicole Richie and Paris Hilton were the trail blazers of socialites filming reality shows and everything worked out for them and it didn't ruin their parents' businesses and careers." I'm proud of the little speech I just made.

"So your argument is that dimwits paved the way for you to embarrass your family on national TV. Are you using again?"

"Whoa, that hurts." My voice trembles. "You will never let that go, will you? Nothing will ever be enough. I can have a picture-perfect family, bring in millions to our corporation, and feed the hungry but to you I'll always be the little girl who liked to party and get high."

"I'm sorry," Brian's says barely above a whisper.

"I know you are not ecstatic about the show, but this is a new generation. Business is not done how Dad is used to anymore. Reality TV, blogs, social media, and cross advertisement with music artists and athletes is how you do business. We have to evolve and bring Ethan Rose and Company into the new ages or get left behind. It's not about being a Z-list celebrity. It's about the bottom line." I pause and Brian is silent.

"Besides," I add, "I'm an executive producer of the show and I have final editing say over every scene I'm in…if that's any consolation," I say as an afterthought.

"That actually makes sense, little sister. We'll see how it goes, but if we get any publicity that negatively affects sales you're done with the show."

We hang up and the corners of my mouth touch my ears. I actually feel good after talking to Brian. He almost sounded disappointed that he didn't think of it first.

I pull up to my destination, a restaurant where I'm meeting Tori, and take my time strolling inside. I have no idea how to handle this. Brian's words ring in my head, so I know all the fighting and arguing I have done on the show so far has to stop and I have to find a way to turn the tables in my favor. My brand depends on it.

I sit at the table across from Tori. My facial expression is stone cold as I cross my arms. "You wanted to talk. Talk."

Tori runs her hands through the long waves draping down her back. I can tell she roller set her hair today. She looks nervous and is bracing herself for the worst. I guess she's a little on edge since I flipped out on her in Miami. I suddenly feel bad. This is just not TV for her. This is her real life that just happens to be playing out on TV. I feel like I'm toying with her. I was a little upset at what she did, but nowhere near as angry as I pretended to be. How could I be when I know Logan doesn't want either of us? I wish I could tell her that I only did that for the cameras to put her at ease, but protecting myself and my family is more important than consoling her.

"I'm sorry," Tori blurts out. "I'm not going to make

any excuses because there are none. I've disrespected you and your marriage and I'm sorry."

"Okay. I accept your apology and I forgive you. I've known you for a while and you've never been malicious. You're just a big ball of crazy butter."

Tori sighs with relief.

"You know it."

We laugh. Tori smiles, gleaming with relief. And I have to admit to myself I'm a little envious of Tori. She has the carefree life I once had. She doesn't have to play pretend. She can live life the way she wants.

"You know why I like you so much?" I continue before she can respond. "You remind me of myself, before I got married, of course."

Tori's smile widens.

"I know you don't want Logan. That's not the problem. The problem is your drinking. You were wasted in Miami. You could have drowned that night because of your drinking." Tori begins to object and I wave my hand, silencing her. "I'm not calling you an alcoholic. I'm just saying slow down before you spiral out of control."

Tori nods her head and I can't tell if my words have gotten through to her.

"Well, you're right. I don't want Logan. I want Blake." She raises her eyebrow and grins at the look of shock that just spread over my face.

"He's black! I didn't think he was your type."

Tori gasps. "Ky, that's racist!"

"That's stating facts. I'm all for the swirl but I've never seen you with a black guy in your life. Heck, I've never seen you with someone of your own race. You've only dated white guys." I mockingly look her up and down. "Why all of the sudden you want a little chocolate in your

156

tea?" I ask, swirling my hips in my seat. "Spill it, honey."

Tori laughs.

"Okay, okay, okay," she says quickly. "So after everything went down that night in Miami, I was a little upset that I possibly lost a friend and I needed a drink." I went to the bar and lo and behold Blake was sitting there all alone and self-loathing over breaking up with THOT."

"THOT?"

"Yes, THOT. That hoe over there." She tilts her head and bucks her eyes and I realize she's talking about Skylar.

"Oh!" I laugh.

"Where was I? Oh, Blake was self-loathing over THOT and I was doing my own self-loathing. So we decided to self-loath together." She starts humping the air. "All. Over. My. Hotel. Room."

"Wow! Did you console him, girl?" I laugh.

"Oh, I consoled him," she replies, still humping the air. "We consoled each other." We laugh together.

I shake my head.

"THOT is going to kill you when she finds out. They just broke up. I know she is hoping to still work it out."

"I don't care," Tori says nonchalantly. "It's not like we're friends, so I'm not breaking the girl code. I really do like him, like a lot. We have been talking every day since Miami and I'm falling for him. He's a winner and I will do what it takes to win him." She winks.

"You are something *else*," I say, emphasizing the else. "Well, girlie, I have to get back to my son and husband."

I stand up and give her a hug. I leave Tori and the cameras behind as I drive home thinking about what she told me. Blake is not slick. I know exactly what he is doing. He's going from one wife to the other so he can stay on the show. He really wants his 15 minutes of shine. I wonder if

Tori really likes him or if their little romance is an arranged agreement between them. She's never so much as glanced at a dude unless he was white. I find it odd that her preference has suddenly changed. I guess it doesn't matter. As long as Blake doesn't breach the morality and confidentially clause of our agreement I don't care what or who he does.

I pull up in my garage and hop out my red Jag. I look over to my Jeep and sneer. I should sell it. It's not like I'll be using it any time soon. Better yet I'll auction it off and send the proceeds to Sophia Tanya Love Thy Children, Bella's charity that aids orphaned children. Brian would love that. I can even film the auction on the show and make a whole event out of it. I put a little pep in my step as I walk inside the house. I'm excited about my auction idea, using a bad situation for good.

"Oh, yes. Jesus, yes! Just like that. Do that tongue swirl thing again," I hear a voice moaning in ecstasy from the living room.

I know it's not what I think. After all the bull Logan gave me earlier about the post-nup, those lovemaking sounds better be coming from Cinemax. I pull my phone out my purse and turn on the video recorder, as extra reassurance to force him into signing the post-nuptial agreement. I tiptoe from the kitchen to the living room. Me and my camera phone peek around the corner. Mario's lying confused ass is standing beside the couch holding on to it for dear life with one hand. His jeans are wrapped around his ankles and as always, his gun with the black handle is lying on the coffee table next to what looks like the post-nup. I can see Logan's signature on the papers from here.

He is holding on to Logan's cropped curls, pushing his

head in and out of his crotch. Logan's knees are pressed into my white rug with his eyes tightly shut, looking like he is enjoying every stroke he is giving Mario with his tongue. Logan's fingers are pressed into Mario's chocolate butt as he swirls his tongue around the tip of his penis before swallowing it whole with his mouth. The TV catches my eye. The house's surveillance of the gate and driveway are on.

Logan wanted me to catch him this time. Since he wants me to watch, I'll watch. I walk around the corner and lean my shoulder against the wall and cross my arms with my phone in my hand as I record. Logan opens his eyes and our eyes meet. Mario is enjoying himself too much to hear me walk in the room.

"I'm cumming! I'm cumming! Daddy's going to cum in your mouth," Mario announces as he begins to thrust harder and quicker in Logan's mouth.

Logan's eyes stay locked onto mine as Mario's body jerks and he grips Logan's curls even tighter.

"You're my bitch. Oh...I'm cumming...ah, ah. Only. You. Can. Make. Me. Feel. This. Good. I love...youuuuu." Logan keeps strumming his penis with his mouth. Mario slumps over and his knees buckle right before pushing Logan's head away from him.

Logan wipes his lips and smiles up at Mario, who is still oblivious to my presence.

"Tell me you love me again," he says

Mario rubs Logan's head. "You know I love you, baby."

"You do?" I speak up. Mario looks back, noticing me for the first time. A look of panic crosses his face. "Because you told me you didn't. You said you were just giving him what he wanted so he would sign with you."

"What?" Logan looks hurt and confused as he gets up off his knees.

"Oh, he didn't tell you?"

"Tell me what?" Logan gently asks, stroking Mario's cheek.

"That the baby I'm carrying is his," I say as I edge toward him." Logan sits on the couch looking dazed. He looks like I just punched him in the face and I take satisfaction that my words hurt him more than his fist could ever hurt me. Mario shakes his head, trying to signal me to be quiet. He already lost me; he doesn't want to lose Logan too.

"Look, I...I can explain," Mario stutters as the words nervously spill from his lips.

"Shut up!" I shout. "Explain to him how you told me you loved me too. Explain to him how we've been having an affair for the last 18 months and you repeatedly begged me to divorce him."

"No, no, no." Logan buries his face into his hands.

"What? You can have an affair, but I can't? Does it hurt you to know the penis you just sucked was all in my vagina? You never wanted to kiss my vagina but I guess you did." I laugh in a condescending tone in Logan's face. Logan yelps out, sounding like a wounded dog.

"Stop it. Just stop it," Mario says. "Why do you have to rub it in? I have enough love for both of you."

He opens his arms like we were both supposed to run into his embrace.

I look at him quizzically.

"Do you? Is that why you threaten me with a paternity and child support suit if I don't keep seeing you behind my husband's back?"

"Umm. Umm," Mario stammers.

Logan cries out in frustration. Agony is in his eyes and tears cover the anger in his face. He reaches for Mario's gun. Instinctively I reach for the gun, trying to get to it before Logan, and so does Mario. The gun explodes and I see a white flash.

14
Glitter and Gold

Angel

"Where are you at? Hello, hello. Angel. I know you're there," Beau starts fussing over the phone before I am even able to say hello. I can imagine the scowl on her face. There is no telling what she is mad about now. Whatever it is, I really am not trying to hear her right now. I have so much that I am dealing with. I hang up, leaving Beau to fuss and argue by herself.

I need to talk to my sisters. I need to talk to someone about everything that has been going on. I have been overwhelmed with drama and I know they will understand, but I will have to get past Beau's fussing first. She is one of those *can't get a word in* type people. She starts going in and doesn't stop until her point is proven and then maybe you'd have a chance to make your argument. I guess that's why she's such a great attorney. At least I know Bella will be more cool. Even when I mess up, Bella tends to be so much easier on me. It's like good cop, bad cop with those two.

I am still trying to wrap my mind around everything. I was almost raped and killed, I murdered a man, and most devastatingly, I was betrayed by my mother. Not to mention that I lost my virginity and had a major argument with Daniel. I went through more in one night than most people go through in a lifetime. God, I am so stressed out. I sit in front of my condo with the car still running, debating on going upstairs. I've been staying at the condo by myself. I am not in the mood to be around anyone, but I don't want to be alone either. I'm so confused.

163

"Ms. Jones?" Felix, the doorman, startles the mess out of me. That quick, I had dozed off, hitting my head on the steering wheel and accidently honking my horn.

"I'm fine, Felix." I crack my window and let him know I don't need anything. I pull away from the condo and head towards the highway. The only bright spot in my life at the moment is that I got the part in the movie. Speaking of which, I need to pick up a revised script. The director's office is about 30 minutes from the condo. I lower the windows and let the fresh cool breeze blow over my face as I speed down the highway, ignoring the vibrations coming from my purse. I know it's Beau, mad that I have ignored and rejected at least five of her repeated calls.

"Some people want it all but I don't want nothing at all if it ain't you, Daniel." I feel tears coming on as I sing along with Alicia Keys.

I have had her on repeat in the car ever since I got back from Miami. I grab some tissues from my purse. Daniel has tried calling me and even popped up at the condo but I can't talk to him. Who am I to think I could ever have a normal happy life? It is selfish of me to lead Daniel on knowing how messed up I am. God, I know I am not perfect, but I have really tried to turn my life around. Alicia starts singing again.

"If I ain't got you," I continue singing out loud as I pull up to the office. I notice some tall, dark, and handsome model type dude smiling and staring at me. I quickly turn my head, hoping he doesn't try…

"Hey, gorgeous," he says, opening my car door for me with flirting eyes like I hoped he wouldn't. Uhh, I know I can't be looking good with bloodshot eyes, windblown hair, and a runny nose. He grabs my hand.

"No hablo ingles." I swat his hand away, scrunching

up my face as I scurry towards the office door, not giving the guy a chance to respond. I don't have time for getting hit on; I just don't. I walk into the building and head for Michael Finese's office.

"Hey, Angel, you okay?" Michael asks as I walk into his office. His face leans sideways as he looks me over with big eyes, inspecting every inch of me. Although I am dressed like a million bucks, my stress, exhaustion, and frustration are written all over me.

"Just allergies. Gotta pick up my other script after I leave here."

I give a fake cough, smile, and then blow my nose, turning on my acting.

"Okay, just checking. Can't have our star not in tip-top shape."

"It is all good, Mike. I am so excited about the movie." This is true and with shooting coming up within the next few weeks I have to get my stuff together.

"You just missed your leading man, Leo. He's tall, dark, and handsome." Mike winks his eye. Aw, man, is that who that guy in the parking lot was? Things may be awkward when I run into him again. "Oh, shoot, I forgot you're taken," he adds. "Oh well. Just make sure you turn on the chemistry for the camera."

"Of course." I seductively smile, rubbing Mike's shoulder with one hand and grabbing the script with the other.

"Girl, you are fine enough to make me think about joining the other team," Mike says and smiles as he walks me to the door.

"I know," I giggle, placing a big wet kiss on his cheek. I quickly skim through the script as I sashay my way to the car. Once back in the car I toss the script onto my buzzing purse and finally pull the phone out. And guess what? It's Beau.

"Really, Angel? You just gon' ignore my calls. This is exactly why we need to talk to you. Are you on your way home? We have been here waiting for you almost two hours!"

"What? Who is we? Where are you?"

"GG, Bella, and I are at your condo. We had to catch a cab from the airport because you wouldn't answer the phone. This is exactly what I am talking about. She is so irresponsible."

Beau stops talking to me to fuss at Bella about me. I can hear Bella telling Beau to give me a break.

"No, she needs to get herself together. Angel? Angel."

I hang up on Beau again. Yes, I do need to talk but not about how Beau thinks I am messing up my life. I need them to help me figure out how to get my happily ever after just like they did. I am on the verge of having my dream career but I want Daniel too. Beau and Bella messed up and still were able to get the men that they loved. I want that too.

I dial Beau back when I pull up in front of the condo. "Where's GG?"

"Asleep now. It took you so long—"

"Meet me downstairs," I cut Beau off. "I need a drink."

"No, I don't want to go have a drink. This isn't a social visit," Beau scoffs.

"Yes we do," Bella yells in the background. "Let's go, Beau. Angel, here we come!"

I feel like my sisters are the only people I can be totally real with. Once I tell them what has been going on I know not even Beau will be able to stay mad at me.

"Hey." I smile when they finally make it down stairs to

the car. Bella is rocking a cute beige romper and her usually curly hair is blown out, falling down to her waist. Beau looks casually chic with a pair of stonewashed jeans, some red heels, and a matching fitted red shirt. Her usually long pressed out tresses are tossed into a curly ponytail.

"Where's your film crew?" Beau asks sarcastically, plopping down into the front seat rolling her eyes as Bella slides in the back with a big grin on her face.

"Not filming today."

I roll my eyes back at Beau. I glance in the rearview mirror. Bella's smile is gone. She looks disappointed. I know deep down Bella would love to be on the show. She would make a great reality television wife.

"Why would you go on television telling my business, Angel? That is so irresponsible. I shouldn't have to walk out of my office to reporters questioning me about my personal business. This can affect not only my personal life but my career too. Not to mention the twins. I thought you had grown up but it is obvious from your recent actions that you haven't. What would make you think it is okay to do a reality TV show? You and Kylie are still up to your same old shenanigans. And what was that you were telling me about dropping out of school less than a year before graduating to be an actress? What in the world are you thinking? You told me you wanted to change your life. Well, that starts with making good decisions. And this guy Daniel...how long have y'all been dating that you and he are trying to get married? You know what? I think you just need to move back home."

Beau talks a mile a minute, not even pausing to take a breath.

I sniffle a bit and dig in my purse for some more tissue.

"Are you done?" I finally talk over her, my voice

cracking. Beau finally looks over at me with concern when she realizes I am crying.

"Hey, hey. What's wrong?" Bella reaches up, rubbing my shoulder. "See, Beau? I told you not to go in on her like that. It's okay, baby. We just want to make sure you are alright."

"I am sorry, love," Beau apologizes. "I know I can be harsh. I am just worried about you."

I talk through tears.

"I didn't say anything about you or my niece and nephew on the show. Skylar brought up your fight with her, trying to throw shade so I went in on her a little bit. And I definitely didn't bring up the DNA stuff. Kylie accidently let something slip, but she never mentioned you. Y'all know how important family is to me. I would never do anything to intentionally hurt y'all."

I can't stop sobbing. Talking about family makes me think of my mother and what she did. I haven't spoken to her since that night. Well, unless you consider the few words I said to her when the bank called me after she tried to cash the check I had given her. The bank manager called to verify the check was legit and I could hear her in the background.

"See, I told you it was okay, puta," she fussed at the bank manager.

"I just had to verify. The check it is for a substantial amount," he tried to reason with her. "Thank you, Ms. Jimenez-Jones."

The banker was ready to hang up, but then I asked him to put my mother on the phone.

"Mamá, Mamá," I called out to her. I could tell she was on the line. I could hear her breathing, but she didn't say anything.

"Mamá, se que estas alli. I hope that money makes you happy because tienes nada mas. You don't have anything left. You don't have a husband, a job, a boyfriend, or a daughter anymore. Did you hear me, Mamá? I am not your daughter. You are nothing to me. The three women you dumped me on in Indiana are my mamas. I will never forgive you for what you did."

I hung up without waiting for her to respond. I don't know what I thought my words would do to her. I hoped maybe she would feel so bad she would leave the money, but she didn't. The check cleared immediately and I cleared my heart of any love I had for that woman.

I pull up to Dugan's bar and by now I am crying and shaking uncontrollably.

"Angel, Angel. Esta bien." Beau holds me in her arms trying to console me and telling me everything is okay.

"No tristeza, no lagrimas. Te amo, mi amor." Bella continues rubbing my shoulders saying she loves me.

"No, it's not. Nothing is okay and maybe it never will be." I continue sobbing as I tell my sisters everything that went down with my mother, Alejandro, Tony, and Daniel. I feel so relieved when I finish talking.

"Well dang, now I do need a drink," Beau laughs. She grabs some tissue and helps clean my face.

"It is going to be alright. Let's go have that drink and figure out what we need to do to get you and Daniel back good."

"We are Joneses and if we don't know anything else we know how to hustle our way out of catastrophe," Bella laughs as we get out the car.

"Okay."

I sniffle one last time then throw on a happy face as we make our way inside the bar. We grab a seat at a booth and

I immediately order drinks for us all. Getting that all off my chest felt good and brainstorming with my sisters has me feeling even better. I decide that there is no way I am going to give up on Daniel.

"Salud," we all toast.

"Well, everything isn't bad news." I finally remember to tell my sisters about the lead role I got in the movie.

"Wow. I am so proud of you. Congratulations," Bella smiles.

"Me too, Angel. I want you to be happy and it sounds like acting makes you happy. Tell us more about the part," Beau inquires.

"Well, I play an aspiring model who sells drugs to other models to make ends meet until she gets her big break."

No sooner than I finish my sentence we all burst out laughing.

"Sounds like a role perfectly made for you." Bella continues laughing. Beau leans over in her seat, unable to stop laughing at the irony of the movie role.

Yeah, I must admit talking to them about it does sound like a hustle we might have embarked on once upon a time.

"I am glad you are having such a good and happy fucking life, because you are trying to ruin mine!" a slurred voice yells from behind me. I turn around and see Elle, her husband, and a camera crew standing there waiting for me to respond. Isaque looks mortified.

"I know you are having an affair with my fiancé. Skylar saw you two at the gala and I know about the $15,000 he gave you. Just because your man cheats on you doesn't mean it is okay to fuck my man, BITCH!" Elle flings whatever white liquor that is in her glass on me, wetting the front of my blouse and my face.

170

"Are you serious?" I jump out of my seat, startling Elle so much she falls back into a table.

Elle is referring to tabloid stories about Daniel cheating after the photo of my mom running upstairs was leaked. I had already killed that lame story. After making arrangements with Alejandro and feeling my mama was safe—at least at that moment—I took her out shopping for clothes and of course the paparazzi snapped all kinds of pics. I let them know my mama was who they saw running from the cameras. A social media blog then wrote an article titled *Angel's Muy Bonita Familia,* talking about how unfair it was that all the women in my family were so gorgeous. The article had pictures of me, Mamá, Belle, and Beau. Beau was pissed as usual but Bella didn't mind and the article was all truth. The women in my family are fine. And when I was questioned on the show about why she ran from the camera the answer was simple.

"My family enjoys their privacy and would like it respected. If and when they want to be on the show they will be."

I deaded that situation.

"Angel!" Beau and Bella both yell as I stand over Elle. I have no intention of hitting her, especially on camera, but I am going to scare the mess out of her drunk, sloppy, messy self. I can see her husband out the corner of my eye frozen and scared of what may happen next. But I am not about to blow his cover or mine. Putting him on blast would also ruin me.

"You are so pathetic and insecure. I don't know what problems you are having in your relationship but don't try to blame me for them."

"No. No. Skylar saw you two talking. Don't try to play innocent. He won't admit anything but I know—"

"No, what you should know is not to take the word of a dishonest money hungry man hopping skank," I cut Elle off. I had already put things in motion to explain my encounter with Isaque after Kylie told me they confronted her. "Did you get the bottle of La Passion with Milania Givenez's autograph?" I continue to hover over Elle. I bought the expensive perfume for myself straight from the fashion mogul, who donated a bottle for the fundraiser at the gala. However, I used the perfume as a way to hustle myself out the situation with Isaque.

"Yes. But—"

"Well your husband paid me that $15,000 which was twice the amount it went for at the auction as a surprise gift for your birthday."

Her birthday was about a month after the fundraiser so it worked out perfectly.

"That is what Skylar saw. He wanted it to be a surprise for you, but look how you have ruined it and made a big deal out of something so innocent. You are wearing it now."

I can smell the sweet perfume. Elle nods her head yes as an expression of embarrassment and shame comes over her face. The look she has is worth the money I spent on the perfume.

"Stop filming." Ashley, the producer that usually works with Elle, walks over. Elle finally stands up. I am sure she is coming over to tell us how great we did. "The police have been called to Kylie's house. There has been a shooting. I don't have any specific information but…"

I walk away gasping for air. Oh my God, I have to get to Kylie. *Please God, let my sister be okay*, I begin to pray. *Let her family be okay.* With eyes full of tears, I walk over to Beau and Bella who had moved to the bar to make sure they weren't on camera.

"Angel, what's wrong?" Bella asks, seeing the fear in my eyes.

"You make sure to tell them they better not put us on the show. I do not consent to it." Beau is looking towards the bar and not at me. She looks up when she doesn't hear me say anything. "I'm for real, Angel—" She finally pauses when she sees my face. "What did I miss? What's going on?"

"We have to go," I say breathlessly. "There has been a shooting at Kylie's house."

I tell them the limited information I have as we peel out of the parking lot and I try to dial Kylie's number. It keeps going to voicemail. The drive to Kylie's seems like an eternity and the street is so full of police cars and news media I have to park almost a block away. The yellow tape and officers in front of their gate denotes that it is a crime scene and we can't get through.

"Angel. Beau. Bella!" I hear Kylie call out exasperatedly. I turn to see her standing by an ambulance.

"Logan. Logan…he's been…he's been shot," she cries out when we finally make our way over to her. "I have to go to the hospital. I need to be with him."

"Mrs. Rose-Beckham, we need to speak with you," a short, round detective that has been standing next to us speaks up.

"Not tonight you won't. Is she a suspect?" Beau begins to question the detective.

"No. I am not saying that. We need to figure out what happened here."

"Well unless you are detaining her as a suspect Mrs. Rose-Beckham will be going to the hospital to be with her husband. She will come to make a statement later," Beau insists.

"Angel, go with her," Beau orders. I had already made up my mind that I was.

"Who are you?" The detective mugs Beau, annoyed with her assertiveness.

"I am Kylie's sister and one of her many attorneys." Beau rolls her eyes as Bella takes my keys and they turn to walk towards my car. "I am sure one of your officers will make sure Mrs. Rose-Beckham gets to the hospital." Beau looks back, cutting her eyes at the detective. "We'll meet you there."

"Um, well yes, of course." He looks dumbfounded. "Right this way."

He escorts Kylie and me to his unmarked car and opens the back door for us. The night is filled with flashing lights and cameras. The sound of the ambulance's siren begins and cuts through all the noise from media reporters and camera flashes. The detective turns on his siren and follows closely behind the ambulance.

"Everything is going to be okay." I grab Kylie's hand, squeezing it tight.

"Okay." Kylie looks over at me. I feel so sorry for my sister. God, please give her the strength to get through this.

* * * * *

"Mrs. Rose-Beckham, your husband is still alive," a tall, slim female doctor walks up to us and says as soon as we come into the emergency room. Kylie's knees get weak and she falls into me and begins shaking. I can tell she is overwhelmed. At the house she was told he wouldn't make it.

"We are prepping him for surgery. He is unconscious and in critical condition but we are going to do everything we can to save him."

174

"Thank you, doctor," I speak for Kylie who stands lethargic and obviously distressed. "Come on, love, let's sit down." I walk us over to some seats in a waiting room.

"Angel, I–I –," Kylie tries to say something. I shush her, leaning her head on my shoulder and patting her curly blonde tresses.

"It looks like everything that glitters isn't gold for the cast of *Sports Wives*," a TV news reporter says on a flat screen television mounted on the wall of the waiting room. "First a fight between Angel Jimenez-Jones and Elle Cowell over an alleged affair Angel had with Isaque Melo, Elle's fiancé. Now breaking news of a shooting at the home of cast mate Kylie Rose-Beckham."

The five or six other people in the room all turn to look at Kylie and me and begin whispering.

"Mrs. Rose-Beckham," the doctor calls out right before I open my mouth to go off and demand the channel be changed. God, how can they report what is going on like it is nothing more than entertainment? I am feeling this show may have been the worst decision of my life and that is saying a lot given all that I have done.

15
Shattered Stars

Kylie

"Mrs. Rose-Beckham? Mrs. Rose-Beckham?" I barely hear a voice calling over all the different thoughts whirling in my head. So much has happened in a matter of hours and after watching that stupid news show I feel dazed all over again. The world knows Logan has been shot. I clutch on to the nearest thing by me to keep from fainting.

"Ouch. Ky. Ky. Kylie, ouch. Kylie, honey. The doctor is here." I realize I'm forcefully clutching Angel's shoulder and the way she is squirming, it must hurt.

I shake my head and tightly clinch my eyes shut so I can think straight. "I'm sorry, Angel." I brush her shoulder. "Yes, doctor?"

Before the doctor says anything, Beau interrupts. I didn't realize she and Bella were here and GG is with them.

"How about we go into the hallway?"

She looks around at the crowd of people in the waiting room. I notice for the first time all eyes are on me and I feel a mounting pressure to behave just right. If I do the wrong thing I will be slandered for weeks by so-called "eye witnesses" and it sickens me that I even have to be aware of something like that.

The doctor, Angel, Beau, and Bella turn to go out in the hallway. I hesitate. I don't want to hear what the doctor has to say. What if Logan is…? Bella looks back at me and notices my hesitation. She walks back to get me and leads me to the hallway. Once out there everyone looks at me and waits for me to ask the doctor the prognosis, but I don't. I stand there silently, not able to lift my eyes off the floor. So

Beau takes the lead.

"What's the status of Logan's condition? How did the surgery go? Is he stable? Can we go see him?" She is talking a mile a minute.

I look up long enough to see a distraught look on the doctor's face and I already know what he is going to say. "I'm sorry but…" I can't hear the rest of his words.

My knees collapse and I begin to fall to the floor but Beau catches me before I hit the ground, just as the *Sports Wives* cameras roll around the corner.

"Is he really dead?" I cry as Beau lifts me up.

"Handle that!" Beau yells at Angel, nodding towards the cameras and Shannon. Angel spins around. Her attention must have been focused on me, because from the furious expression on her face it seems like she just noticed them for the first time.

I bury my face in Beau's shoulder.

"Please, tell me he's not dead."

Beau rubs my curls. "Sweetie, he's gone."

I cry out in agony. Over my sobbing I hear Angel screaming at the top of her lungs.

"What's wrong with you soulless pieces of shit? We didn't clear this for filming! Nobody wants you here!"

"That's for Kylie to decide if she wants to film this. This is her life. We are just trying to tell her story. Kylie, do you—?"

Before Shannon can finish asking me her question Beau, Bella, Angel, and even GG go off, verbally attacking Shannon. They are all going off at the same time so viciously I can't tell who is saying what or what is even being said. I can barely make out some don't you talk to hers and how dare yous. I keep my head buried in Beau's shoulder, but I can feel her movement and I can tell she is wagging her finger and rolling her neck. I don't think Shannon got a word in before the doctor stepped in and hushed the Jones sisters and GG.

I hear the doctor tell Shannon, "You are creating a disturbance. I have to ask you to leave."

I hear the clatter of what must be Shannon's heels and the camera crew leaving. My head still hasn't left Beau's shoulder and her blouse is soaked through from my tears. She rubs my back and then I feel more hands rubbing my back.

Once I can't hear the clatter anymore I stop hiding my face in Beau's shoulder. I feel sick and I run to the nearest trashcan and throw up. I think my nausea stems from the pregnancy more then what happened with Logan. Then it dawns on me.

"Ethan! Where's my baby? Did anyone call my nanny?" I pat my pockets for my cell phone and turn up empty-handed. "Where's my cell phone? Where's my purse?" I feel like I'm mentally breaking. This is just too much to handle right now. I slide to the floor, tears pouring down my face. "Somebody bring me my baby. I need my purse." My whole body is shaking, almost convulsing.

GG stands over me sternly griping my shoulders. "Get a hold of yourself. You have to be strong for your babies. You can't be falling all over the floor and stuff. I hear you're carrying; you don't want to have a miscarriage because of stress, do you? I know it's tough—Lawd, I know—but you have to be stronger, sweetie pie."

I nod my head.

"Now, Bella has your purse, honey. She can call the nanny for you."

"Ky, what's your passcode?" Bella asks.

"No!" Everyone seems startled at my reluctance. "Just

hand it to me. I want to talk to her myself."

I pause. The video of Logan is on there. I never got a chance to delete it. I only recorded it to pressure him into signing the post-nup, but once I saw he signed the papers I decided that I didn't need it. And now that he's gone I definitely don't want anyone to see that video.

"I want to hear Ethan's voice. It's the only part of Logan that I have right now," I blurt out, not knowing what else to say to keep Bella from accidently stumbling across the video. Everyone's eyes look like their hearts just melted. Bella hands me my phone and I feel relieved. I call the nanny and I tell her Logan was killed and I need her to bring Ethan to the hospital. I have her put Ethan on the phone and I put him on speaker.

"Hi, Mommy." His voice is so innocent. He has no idea how his life just changed and I feel horrible.

"Hi, munchkin. Guess what? All your aunties and GG are here. Say hi."

I am hoping it will help if he knows how much he is loved.

"Hi!" his little squeaky voice says.

"Hi," they all say in unison except for GG who says, "Hey, baby."

I have Ethan put the nanny back on the phone and I make sure she is en route to the hospital. Talking to my baby calms me. GG is right. I gotta do what I got to do for my babies.

After I hang up the phone I make sure to quickly delete the recording. I already made a decision that I don't want Logan's name slandered. I will take Logan's secrets to the grave, starting with destroying that video.

"Doctor," GG says. He never left the hallway. "I know you're busy, but you need to check on Kylie's womb. This is a lot for her and we need to make sure that baby is okay."

"Before you do I want to see Logan, before Ethan gets here."

I need to see his body. The doctor nods and leads us to Logan. They already put his body in the hospital's morgue.

"It's only been five minutes since he passed and you already tossed him aside," Angel sneers.

"Angel, stop. I'm sure it's procedure," Bella chides. I know the doctor must be frightened of saying the wrong thing after witnessing Shannon being verbally ripped to shreds because he high tailed it out of there with the excuse of giving us privacy without addressing Angel's comment.

I slowly approach Logan's body. I have to admit I'm a little scared, like he is going to pop up and yell out *boo*. I run my fingers through his short-cropped curls. Tears running down my face, I graze my fingers over the side of his face. His skin is already going pale. Then I'm overcome with anger and pity for myself. Everything he put me through during our marriage runs through my head. I slap his face as hard as I can.

I scream and repeatedly hit Logan's body.

"What am I supposed to do now?! How am I supposed to get out of this?! What now? What now?" My entire face is wet from tears and I know it's red because it feels warm from blood rushing to it.

Angel immediately grabs one of my arms to stop me from hitting Logan, but I yank away from her while continuing to hit Logan with my other hand. Bella grabs me by the waist. I can hear her and Angel telling me to stop.

"Let her get it out," I hear GG telling them. "It's a part of the grieving process."

"GG, this can be considered desecration of a dead body," Beau objects.

They literally drag me out of there kicking and screaming. As soon as they get me out the room I see Logan's mother rampaging down the hallway.

"You couldn't call me about my only son, you harlot!" Nancy screams at me.

Angel steps in her path before she can get to me.

"Mrs. Beckham, I'm sorry for your loss. We are all grieving here. It's no reason to call Kylie names," she tries to reason with her.

"Hogwash! I don't care how much that skinny stick whoops and hollers and falls all over the place. I know she had something to do with my baby's death and I'm going to wring her neck."

She jumps at me. Beau, Bella, and Angel push her back before she can get to me.

"With all due respect we will not be doing that today," Bella snaps.

"She is going to try to keep me away from my grandbaby," Nancy says, still trying to jump at me, but the sisters are blocking her.

"GG, get Kylie out of here," Beau instructs GG over the racket of Nancy yelling about how she wants to kill me.

"Come on, baby. Let's go find the doctor to get that womb checked out," GG says, leading me away.

The doctor checks me out and thank God my baby is okay. He does tell me I need to find a stress outlet because if I keep stressing it will affect the baby. Just as I am walking out of the examination room the nanny finally arrives with Ethan and I run to him and give him the biggest hug I have ever given him in all his two years of life. I release the nanny from duty. She gives me her condolences and leaves after she sets Ethan's car seat next to me.

Then reality slaps me. It hadn't crossed my mind until now that I have to somehow explain to Ethan what's going on. I have no idea how to tell a two-year-old that his daddy is never coming back. Despite what we were going through as husband and wife, Logan loved his son and Ethan loved him too. I decide to let Ethan have at least one more night of childlike bliss while I contemplate how to tell him this life altering news.

The sisters come to the waiting area, where I'm sitting with Ethan and GG. GG is holding my hand.

"Well, we finally got Mrs. Beckham to calm down for now," Angel says, rubbing her forehead. She looks drained of all energy. "I think we should get Kylie out of here before Ms. Beckham gets turned back up. She's a handful."

"My husband," I hear my own voice saying. "My husband's been shot!" Confused, I look up to the TV where my voice is coming from. They are playing my 911 call on the news.

"How did they even get that so quickly?" Bella asks.

The short round detective that was at my house walks over to us.

"Kylie, we need to take you in for questioning. This is now a murder investigation."

"I'm going," Beau and Angel both say simultaneously.

"No, I need to do this by myself."

If I bring Beau it will seem like I'm lawyering up. I will look suspicious before I get one word out. They need answers from me that only I can provide since I was there when he was murdered.

"Well at least let me drive you," Angel says, not really wanting to leave me alone. I agree and we all begin to walk out of the hospital.

"Don't let them corner you or turn your words around

with their line of questioning," Beau whispers to me as she helps me set up Ethan's car seat in Angel's car.

I know even though the police denied it I'm already a suspect. The spouse is always a suspect in these types of situations.

"I won't. I have the truth by my side," I assure Beau. Out of the corner of my eye, I see Angel running towards Daniel. Before she can hug him he grabs her by her waist, stopping her. A confused frown covers her face.

"Wait. I have to do this first," Daniel tells Angel. Daniel walks over and bear hugs me.

"I'm so, so sorry," he says. "I came as soon as I heard. Are you okay? That's a stupid question. Don't answer. Let me know if there is anything I can do for you."

I nod my head and thank him. He goes back to Angel.

"Okay, now I can." He tightly hugs Angel and kisses her so passionately that it reminds me of the love I had for Logan before we got married.

"I don't know why we are fighting, but I don't want to anymore. I'm sorry," Daniel confesses to Angel.

"Me too. I love you so much," Angel says, still hugging Daniel.

"I love you too." They kiss again. I smile despite my pain. If my situation is what brings them back together then I'm happy for them.

"Okay, cut it with the mushy stuff. Untie your tongues and let's go," Bella interjects.

"Umph," GG grunts, "Just out here all slobber-facing and whatnot."

"GG! Stop!" Beau chides and we all laugh. Angel explains to Daniel that we are on our way to the police station.

"Let me drive you," Daniel offers. "You all can't fit in

Angel's car."

"We're riding along too," Beau and Bella insist.

GG drives Angel's car and takes Ethan with her to Angel's condo and we all cram into Daniel's car. On the way to the police station, Beau insists I go over my statement with her and gives me tips on which wording to use.

When we arrive at the police station I'm nervous but I try to walk in with confidence. The frumpy, short detective leads me to a small room and leaves. In the middle of the room is a metal table with a folding chair on each side of it. I sit down and I look around while I impatiently wait for what seems like forever. The room smells musty from the dank walls. There is no two-way mirror like you see in the movies. Only four walls painted the ugliest shade of yellow I've ever seen. I dab my eyes that are quickly filling up with tears and continue to look around to see if there are any cameras. I don't see one. I wonder if they are somehow monitoring me right now. I check my cell phone and almost 30 minutes have passed. I start to feel disrespected at how long they are making me wait. I get up and make my way to the door when it suddenly flies open.

"I'm glad you could finally make it, but I'm leaving," I tell the woman dressed in black slacks, a cheetah print button up cotton blouse with the sleeves rolled up to her elbows, and a black vest.

"Sorry for your wait. I was in the middle of an interrogation when you arrived. I'm Detective Robinson." She sticks her hand out for me to shake but I just look at it and sit down.

"Before we jump in, I need to inform you this conversation will be recorded and I need you to sign this waiver of consent."

I nod my head at Detective Robinson. She slides a piece of paper and pen over to me as she places a small voice recorder in the middle of the table. I notice she didn't press any buttons to turn it on. She had the recorder on before she came into the room and I realize how serious this is.

I look over the paper labeled CONSENT as I listen to the detective explain to me what it is.

"You are currently not being detained and are free to go at any time. Any statement you give today is of your free and voluntary will. Are you under the influence of drugs or alcohol?" I shake my head no. "Please, speak out loud for the recorder."

"No, I'm not," I say as I sign the paper, never looking up at her.

Detective Robinson takes a deep breath.

"Well, we're ready to begin here. Tell me everything you know."

I look up at the detective, remembering what Beau taught me on the way over here.

"You have to be more specific. I don't know where to begin."

"Well, let's begin with who shot your husband." Detective Robinson studies my face as tears fill my eyes.

"Mario."

Donisha Derice & Jai Darlene

16
Too Real to be Scripted

Angel

"Get over here." Daniel pulls me back onto the bed and starts kissing me on my lips, quickly moving down to my neck as his hands caress my butt. To say things are good with us is an understatement. Through everything that has been going on with my family Daniel has been there and refused to leave my side.

"Stop. I gotta go," I giggle. As much as I'd love to stay in bed with him all day Kylie and I have a meeting with the producers. I can't believe they won't agree to cancel the rest of the season after what happened to Logan. They temporarily postponed shooting to give Kylie time to "grieve" and plan the funeral but then they had the audacity to ask if they could film the funeral services. I know I need to keep my cool but I get mad every time I think about those shady people.

"Mrs. Silver, please be on your best behavior."

Daniel sits up in bed staring at me with his golden eyes as I slip off my wedding band and place it in the night stand drawer. Daniel and I had managed to quietly get married about a month ago without anyone finding out. After Logan died we both knew we didn't want to waste another moment apart. Life is so fragile I know I have to hang on to what I have and seize every moment. It is still surreal thinking about it and Daniel loves calling me Mrs. Silver when we are alone. I still want my big wedding ceremony with my amazing Vera Wang gown, but I know it isn't the right time for that or to tell anyone we are already married.

"I promise." I kiss Daniel before rushing off to get

ready. Everything is finally going right for me. Daniel and I are happy. The movie shoot is complete, and the movie will be released soon. And Kylie is doing better. I cannot imagine going through what she had been through. I shake my head as I hop in my Range Rover and drive to Meskerem Ethiopian restaurant for the meeting.

* * * * *

"Hey, Angel, thank you for meeting with us." Evan pulls out a seat for me. Kylie is already there and so is Shannon and the executive producer, Kurt Matthews.

"Would you like something to drink?" he asks.

"No," I curtly reply.

"Look, we understand your position on this, but filming will continue. There aren't that many episodes left." Kurt gets right down to business. His orange tan, pearly whites, and annoying scratchy voice are getting on my nerves already.

"I don't need you to recap the shooting schedule. I am well aware of it. What I don't understand is how after everything my sister has been through you expect us to continue. You cold-hearted—"

"Angel, it's okay. Let's just finish the season. I am fine, okay?" Kylie interjects.

"No, it is not. This is definitely not okay," I retort.

"Reality TV is just that—reality. And in real life tragedy happens, but we have to keep going and that includes going to work. You have a contractual obligation to finish this season," Kurt continues to annoy me.

"Really, that is all you have to say? Y'all make me sick."

I stand up and slam the chair into the table. If I am required to finish this season I will do it, but they can forget about me coming back for another season. I storm to the bathroom and hear Kylie's heels click-clacking right behind me.

I run into a bathroom stall and drop to my knees.

"Let me help you." Kylie locks the bathroom door.

"Oh my God, why didn't you warn me about this morning sickness stuff?" I hurl into the toilet.

"Oh my God! Are you pregnant? Welcome to the wonderful world of motherhood." Kylie laughs as she holds my hair back. I release the 7UP and crackers I nibbled on this morning into the toilet.

"Have you told Daniel yet?" Kylie asks once I finally get up and go to rinse my mouth out.

"No. I am just waiting for the right time. I mean everything is finally on track with us and I don't want this to....you know."

I look up at Kylie through the mirror and see her big blue eyes empathizing with me. She is now a pregnant widow. I know she understands how things can quickly go bad.

"Enough about me. How are you doing? I can't believe they are talking about contracts and stuff. Look, I can get Beau to go over our contracts and figure out how to get us out of this."

"No, Angel, I need this show." Kylie looks at me. What does she mean she needs this show? Is she crazy? "Our family and this show are the only things keeping me sane. Like they said, this is our job. If I didn't have to work what would I be doing? I'll tell you. I'd be somewhere cooped up in the house balling my eyes out. But I can't do this without you. Promise me you won't leave the show." Kylie pokes out her lip and gives me the puppy dog eyes.

"Okay," I reluctantly agree. I will do just about anything to make sure she is okay.

"Anyway, I am so excited. I can't wait for our girls to be born. They are going to be the best of friends just like us." Kylie already has it made up in her mind that we are both having girls. "Are you ready to go back out there?"

"No, not really. Tell them I agree to finish the season. Then get rid of them, please." I smile and give Kylie a hug. "I'll be out in a second."

Kylie walks out of the bathroom and I stare at myself in the mirror. I am going to tell Daniel about the baby tonight. I don't know what I'm worried about. I am sure he will be elated. Oh and a little girl would be so cute and perfect. I close my eyes, imaging what she might look like.

"Angel, honey." Kylie walks back into the bathroom with a look of concern on her face.

"Dang, what else do they want? I said I will finish the season. I don't want to hear about season two right now."

"No, no, ESPN just broke some news about Daniel."

"What? Is something wrong? Is he okay?"

"No, honey, Daniel is okay, but—"

"But what? Ky, tell me what is going on."

"They just reported that Daniel is the father of Savannah Winter's newborn son."

"What? Whatever. It's just some media publicity stunt."

I head out of the bathroom, unfazed by what Kylie just said. Daniel and I have been together for a year now. There is no way he is the father of that child.

"Angel, no, wait!" Kylie tries to grab my shoulder, but is too late. I walk back into the restaurant, which is now full of cameras, including the show's film crew. Kylie steps in front of me, trying to shoo them out the way.

"Angel, how do feel about Daniel having a baby with his ex?" A female reporter shoves a mic past Kylie and into my face.

"He doesn't have a baby. This is the first I have heard about this, but I am sure that my fiancé has not been cheating on me."

"But the DNA results are conclusive. Dennis Silver, Daniel's father, gave a DNA sample and this baby is definitely a Silver. He is Daniel's child," the reporter continues.

I stop in my tracks. Feeling light headed, I grip a chair. The room is spinning and then it gets dark.

* * * * *

"Ms. Jones?" I feel a gentle nudge. When I open my eyes I see a paramedic standing over me taking my blood pressure. Kylie is sitting to my left.

"Angel, we are on our way to the hospital. We have to make sure you and the baby are okay," Kylie says, running her fingers through my hair to try to comfort me.

"Ms. Jones, how far along are you? Do feel any abdominal pressure or pain? How about your vision? Is it blurry?" Do you suffer from any medical conditions? Heart problems, asthma, cancer?"

I try to answer all of the medic's questions and as soon as we arrive at the hospital I am hooked up to monitors and asked a million more.

"Please, God, let my baby be okay," I pray grabbing Kylie's hand to pray with me. I am so scared I keep watching the door waiting for the doctor. I need to know that everything is alright. When the doctor finally walks in he is smiling. I take it as a sign of good news. "Doctor, please tell me my baby is alright," I say before the doctor can even speak.

"Yes." He smiles. "The baby is doing great and so is mommy. The stress of the news you received made you faint. Ms. Jones, as I am sure you understand you need to do your best to alleviate any stress that you may have in your life. For you and most importantly the baby's sake, you have to take care of yourself." The doctor lets me know they need to keep me for a few more hours for observation and then I will be released.

"Thank God," Kylie exhales. "I am going to call Daniel. He has been blowing my phone up."

"No!" I snatch the phone out of her hand and sit up in the bed. "Turn the TV on," I order Kylie. I need to hear the truth for myself.

"No, Angel, please." I stare Kylie dead in her eyes until she reluctantly turns the TV on. As suspected, Daniel and I are breaking news. They keep replaying the DNA story and me fainting at the restaurant.

"I hope Daniel has a damn good explanation for this," Kylie says, screwing up her face.

"What explanation can there be? Either he is the father or he is not, and if he is, I am done. Simple as that."

"Angel," I hear Daniel call out to me from the door. His golden eyes are dim and bloodshot red like he has been crying. "Kylie, can you give us a minute?" he asks

"No. Kylie, stay." I grab her hand as I glare at Daniel. His cologne, his voice, everything about him is infuriating me.

"Babe, I was so worried about you." I smush Daniel's face with my hand as he leans in to give me a kiss.

"Don't touch me." I don't try to hide the look of disgust written all over my face. "How could you do this to us?"

"I have never cheated on you."

"Then he's not your baby?" I probe Daniel's face, waiting for his answer. Every news media outlet has reported conclusively that he is. I can never trust Daniel again and I don't really think his answer matters.

"Yes, but—"

"But what?!" my voice raises to a yell.

"I don't know how—"

"You don't know how? Usually a man sticks his penis in a woman's vagina." My voice continues to get louder.

"Angel, you have to believe me. I just found out about the baby today just like you. Savannah and I—"

"Get out!" I scream at the top of my lungs as I fling the hospital phone at Daniel's head. It crashes into the wall. Daniel has a bewildered look on his face like he doesn't understand why I am so upset.

"Get out!" I scream again, this time flinging my cell phone at him. He catches it before it hits the wall.

"Daniel, you have to go now," Kylie jumps in.

"Angel, no. Don't do this." Daniel looks at me with desperation in his eyes.

"Get out!" Kylie yells before I am able to. A doctor and nurse rush into the room to check on the commotion. *Leave*, Kylie silently mouths to Daniel.

"Angel, I need you." Kylie shoves Daniel out of the room before he can finish his sentence.

The tears run from my face like a river. Kylie steps out the room, leaving the door open and I ask the nurse to turn the lights off and close the door behind her. This cannot be real life. If I wasn't here right now living this I'd swear it was all scripted. But this right here, my life right now, is too real to be scripted.

Donisha Derice & Jai Darlene

17
Fade To Black

Kylie

"Holy Mother of Jesus! You can't be serious!" I scream at Daniel as I storm after him with the *Sports Wives* cameras in tow right after I kicked him out of Angel's hospital room. The cameras were there when the news about Daniel's secret love child broke, they were there when Angel fainted from hearing the news, they were there when the ambulance carted her off to the hospital, and they were waiting anxiously outside her hospital room.

Evan and Shannon tried to actually come into the room with the cameras, but Angel was not having it. She hasn't told anyone about her pregnancy, including Daniel, and I'm sure that's part of the reason why she insisted on not allowing them to film her in the hospital. Well, that and the fact that she hates their guts.

Daniel turns to look at me, exasperated. His eyes are bloodshot. He looks like he's about to cry. That's what he gets.

"How dare you?!" I push his shoulder. "How long?!" I ask, still screaming.

"What?" Daniel looks around at the camera crew uncomfortable to be having this conversation, knowing it's being filmed. I keep focused on him, but out of the side of my eye I see Evan with a huge grin, loving every minute of the confrontation.

"Don't play stupid. How long have you been cheating?"

I'm not buying into his lies that he told Angel and thank God neither is she. I am determined to get answers

196

for her since she can't get them herself without going into emotional overdrive and harming her unborn child.

"I'm not going to do this with you. I don't owe you any answers, only Angel." Daniel turns his back on me and walks away.

"Be a man and own up to your treachery!" I yell. "I was rooting for you two and this is how you treat her."

My words stop Daniel in his tracks.

"There was no treachery! I need you to help Angel believe that."

"You got another woman pregnant while you were supposed to be in love with Angel," I scoff. "That is the definition of treachery. And you want me to convince Angel to abandon all common sense in the name of love? Screw you and screw love."

If I had something to throw at him I would right now.

"What do you want? You want Angel to be a big happy family with you and your concubine? She'll never forgive you because forgiving you means she has to accept your child. A living and breathing reminder of your dogness. Is that want you want?"

"All I know is that I want Angel. I love her more than you will ever understand."

A tear escapes from Daniel's eye. He turns around and hurries down the hallway. This time I don't follow him. He sounds so convincing, but I just can't believe him. He cheated and the world knows. There's no hiding from that. There's no way Angel can pretend that everything is okay between them when the world already knows. If I was Angel I would die from embarrassment.

"Cut!" Shannon yells. "Oh my gosh! That was great. No, amazing. You can't write this stuff!" Before I can even get a word in she continues. "Now all you have to do is convince Angel to let us in the room. The viewers will want to see how she is doing."

Fuck you and the viewers, is what I want to say, but she has a point. I sigh.

"The doctor is going to release her soon. Maybe she'll agree to film after she is released to recap what just happened."

"Awesome. Do that." Shannon beams. I roll my eyes and go back into Angel's room, making sure to close the door behind me.

"So what's the word, doc? Can she go home now?" I ask.

"I just cleared her to go home. Angel, remember you have to keep your stress levels down," the doctor says before leaving the room.

"Angel, listen. Shannon wants to film us leaving the hospital."

"Tell her no," Angel says matter-of-factly. "The doctor just said I need to keep my stress levels down. I'm not going to let Shannon and that show stress me out."

I nod my head and contemplate my next words carefully. "Filming in itself won't stress you out, Angel. The only reason why you don't want to film is to maintain some type of privacy. But the cameras already captured everything. They saw you break down when the news broke about Daniel. So at this point you have two choices. You can film and tell the story you want to tell or let them tell it for you. The blogs are already going crazy. Rumors are running rampant and that's what's going to stress you out—dealing with the rumors and the media—so you might as well just tell your side of the story and silence them all." Angel sits quietly for a few seconds and I'm pretty sure she is thinking over what I just told her. "So what's it going to

198

be?"

Angel huffs. "Fine. But not one word about the baby," she makes me promise.

"Of course not. I'm going to help you settle in at home. We'll have some girl time and discuss what you believe to be the truth and your feelings. Is that okay?" Angel nods her head in agreement as she gets out of the bed. She is still in her street clothes. We walk out the room and I nod at Shannon to indicate that it's go time. The cameras instantly light up and follow us out the hospital.

Once in my car, I dial my house phone to call GG. She never left. She helped me make the arrangements for Logan's cremation and funeral. Then she stayed to help me with Ethan. I only want family around; no nannies, no maids, no cooks, just family. And I really need the help. Ethan is a handful. He cries nonstop for his daddy and it breaks my heart. I'm so grateful for GG. She's not actually related to me by blood but she has always treated me like I am one of her own. She's always embraced me just like my mother always embraced Bella. But I just wished my mother would show me that same love. I'm constantly feeling like an outcast in my own family just because I don't do things the way she thinks I should.

"Hello, Kylie," I hear my mother's voice through the car's speakers.

"Mom?" Angel and I look at each other shocked. "What are you doing here?"

"I flew down on the jet so we can chat. I don't like the way we ended things before I left."

When my mother flew down here for the funeral, her first words to me when she saw me were not *how are you doing*, *are you okay*, or *honey, I love you.* Her first words were, *I'm not being filmed on your little reality show, am I?*

And everything went downhill from there. We argued about my appearance on the show until she left. I had Ethan crying in one ear and my mother nagging me in the other. I never got the chance to process my feeling about Logan's death. I was on the verge of a mental breakdown and I asked her to go. I love my mother but I couldn't handle the stress of arguing with her anymore. I've come to the conclusion that I just have to prove to her that this is a good direction for our family's corporation with results and not with my words.

"Mom, I'm not going to stop filming the show if that's what you came down here for. I've already told you a million times that I made the commitment and I can't take it back. I've already filmed too much of the show."

"I'm not here to talk you out of the show. I'm here to show my support for you. I've been way too hard on you. I'm still skeptical but maybe Bella is right; maybe I'm being old school. This reality show might be the new way of marketing and building brand recognition."

I am at a loss for words. Bella must have talked some sense into my mother, like I talked sense to Brian.

I am overwhelmed with a flood of emotions.

"Mom..."

"Honey, you don't need to say anything. Just know I'm here for you. Now, GG told me Angel was rushed to the hospital. How is she?"

She reminds me why I am calling in the first place. Earlier I called GG to tell her that Angel fainted and was on the way to hospital. I know she must be worried.

"She's fine. I'm taking her home now and I think GG should look after her. I'm sending a car for her now."

We hang up and I feel grateful that my mom is here to support me.

I pull up to Angel's condo and the camera crew follows us inside. Angel turns on her TV when we walk through the door. Angel plops on the couch and I snuggle up next to her. Big as day the words BREAKING NEWS flash in bold red letters across the bottom of the screen. I don't know why Angel continues to torture herself, but she turns up the volume and watches as a thick blonde-haired, blue-eyed woman takes a podium. I can't help but to think about Savannah, although the woman on TV doesn't resemble her at all other than the obvious fact that they are both white. Savannah is a pretty, petite, long-legged redhead debutant from none other than Savannah, Georgia. I have never met her but we have been at the same place at the same time before. She is a socialite that keeps her perfectly manicured fingers into a little bit of everything in Georgia.

"I am with the office of Lewis, Williams, and Council and I represent Daniel Silver. Upon receiving news of the birth of the child of Savannah Winters and the DNA test results indicating that our client Daniel Silver is the father of this child, a three-month-old boy, our office, with the assistance of a private investigator, has begun to delve into this matter. Although this is only the start of our investigation, we have already come across a source of information indicating that this child was not born of a sexual relationship and encounter between Ms. Winters and Mr. Silver." The thick blonde takes a dramatic pause. If not from a sexual encounter than from what? I impatiently wait for her to continue. "Upon the conclusion of our investigation there will be evidence to prove that Ms. Winters' child was conceived through at-home artificial insemination using sperm previously acquired while Ms. Winters and Mr. Silver were dating."

"Yeah right!" I roll my eyes and snatch the remote from Angel, turning the TV off without waiting to listen to the question and answer portion of the press conference.

We sit in silence for a moment. The cameras make it awkward for us to let our guard down and talk. Besides, I don't know what to say. *Sorry that the love of your life, your baby daddy, your future husband, the man you gave your virginity to, had a baby with someone else and it's being played out all over the media for the world to see.*

I finally speak up. "You must be mortified."

"I thought our love was real," her voice quivers. I know the tears will come soon. She won't be able to hold them back for much longer. I know she wants to put on her mask for the cameras but this is too real.

"He said he didn't know how she got pregnant. You don't believe that, do you?"

Tears roll down her face and she gives a grimacing laugh.

"I don't know what to believe. He's saying he didn't. His attorney said she was artificially inseminated, but how do you have a baby and not know how it happened?"

"Artificial or not, what's worse is that the chick knew he was engaged and she still went after him. Thots are running amuck and nobody's man is off limits. They don't care if they are not the main chick as long as they get fed a little bit of the scraps. Scrappy hoes."

Angel shakes her head.

"*His* loyalty should have been to me. She doesn't have to be loyal to me. She doesn't even know me. But I expected him to do better."

"So what are you going to do?"

"I'm going to work on healing my heart and building my movie career."

"So does that mean you're not going to try to work it out with Daniel?"

Angel responds by sobbing and putting her head on my shoulder. I can see the cameras zooming in on her pain. The whole situation baffles me. They seemed so in love, but I know better. Things on the surface are never what they seem.

I think back to the day when Logan repeatedly shoved my head in the toilet. I remember Angel had a smile on her face but her eyes told a different story. She probably knew about the cheating and the baby then. I believe that artificial insemination story is just a cover up by Daniel to save face to the public. No wonder Angel caved and had sex with Daniel when she always swore she wouldn't have sex until marriage. She was probably trying to keep him, maybe even get pregnant on purpose to compete with Daniel's side piece. And when his cheating broke national news it was probably too much for her and she fainted in embarrassment.

Gosh, I hope I'm wrong, but what else could she be hiding if that isn't it? I hope she didn't make a bad situation worse by getting pregnant on purpose to keep Daniel. I swear I could kill Daniel for what he is putting Angel through. I squeeze Angel as she sobs on my shoulder. The more I think about it the more pissed I get. These men treat us like dirt and we just take it as women. Logan dragged my heart through the mud, over razor blades, and left it to soak in a puddle of alcohol. But yet I still feel the need to protect his image, even in his death. I wish I would have never lied to the police about his sexuality. I should just tell the truth about Logan, but I can't. I decide after I leave Angel's I will go to the priest and confess the sins I've committed.

BANG, BANG, BANG, BANG, BANG, BANG!

Angel and I jump as my thoughts are interrupted by rapid banging on the door.

"Who's that?" I ask, looking over at Shannon and Evan for any clues on their faces as to who it might be at the door.

"I don't know. I have no idea, but they're knocking like they are the freaking police!" Angel shouts and gets up and answers the door. GG is standing at the door in mid-knock. I forgot she was on her way. She got here quick.

"How's my baby?" GG asks, giving Angel a big hug.

"I'm glad you're here. I need my GG," Angel cries into her shoulder.

"Yes, you also need a bath and to wash your hair or something. You too pretty to be looking like this on camera. You look like a little sick poodle," GG lightens the mood. I laugh. GG is right. Angel's hair does look a tangled mess.

"GG, you're right. I'm not going to sit around here moping. Let's go get our hair done," Angel suggests.

"Oooh, I want to go film that. Kylie, do you mind? You don't have anything interesting to shoot, do you?" Shannon asks.

"Nope. I'm going home to be with my son." I hug Angel and GG goodbye, grab my purse, and walk to my car in the parking garage.

As soon as I pull out my parking space, red and blue lights circle around my car. I'm so startled I hit the curb before slamming on my breaks.

A police officer quickly runs up to my car, his face blocked by the barrel of his gun that is aimed at my head. "Put your hands in the air! Put your hands in the air right now!" he barks at me. Confused and afraid, I slowly raise my hands.

"What's going on?" my voice quivers.

Detective Robinson walks up to my car. She is dressed in jeans, a black T-shirt, and a bulletproof vest with her police badge hanging over it.

"You're under arrest for the murder of Logan Beckham."

18
The Camera's Almost Always Rolling

Angel

"GG, are you ready?" I quickly cover my mouth when I realize how loud I am. I have to get out of this condo before I go crazy. Evan and Shannon keep giving play by play of the media's coverage of the Savannah and Daniel ordeal, including the fact that Savannah's car has been parked at Daniel's mansion all afternoon.

"Chile, I might be old but I ain't deaf," GG fusses with her brows scrunched together, mugging me as she makes her way to the front door of the condo.

I need her here with me. With what Beau and Bella went through being alone and pregnant I know my GG is not about to let me go through this alone. I shudder at the irony that each of us have had issues with our men as we have gone through our pregnancies.

"Sorry, just that the car is being pulled up front and I still need to check the mail," I state softly to GG as we head to the elevator.

"Oh, wow." I mug my reflection in the mirror. GG was not lying about me needing to do something with my hair. I hopped in the shower but didn't bother to fool with my hair since we are going to the beauty salon anyway. It looks like a matted lion's mane.

I grab the mail, stuff it into my purse, and pause as I look outside.

"Damn reporters," I mumble, debating on running back up to my condo and hiding out.

I turn to see Evan, Shannon, and my own film crew following close behind me. I flash an irritated smile. It won't be any better being cooped up in the condo with them trying to pry a scene out of me.

"What you say, baby?" GG wraps her arms around my waist, giving me a side hug. I turn to take on her full embrace. I hold on to her, enjoying her warmth.

"It is going to be okay, baby," GG whispers in my ear and then plants her soft lips on my cheek.

"I love you," I whisper back.

"I love you too. Now let's go get this hair did." She pats the mess on top of my head.

I take deep breath and head straight to my Maserati waiting for us up front.

"ANGEL! ANGEL! ANGEL!" I ignore the reporters shouting my name but throw on my Prada shades and smile big and bright for the cameras. Hopefully my Kool-Aid smile will distract from the bush on top of my head.

"Ouch." My fingers get stuck as I try to comb through my hair after I get in the car.

"Maybe, baby, you should have worn a hat," GG laughs, patting me on the head.

"GG!" A real smile flashes across my face for the first time this afternoon. She is right, though. I look at her as she sits in the passenger's seat. My GG looks good for her age. She could be the poster child for the saying 'Black don't crack.' Her silver hair in its usual tight curls is beautiful, her almond-shaped eyes remind me of my sisters' and mine, and she has that killer smile she passed down to my dad and us too. Built like a little brick house, GG is definitely what I want to look like when I grow up.

"So GG, my good Judie is going to hook your hair up. You promised you would get it blown out. It is going to be so pretty."

"Oh baby, you know you don't have to do all this for me," GG blushes.

"But I want to, GG. You are everything to me and I just want to show you some appreciation. Plus I need something to take my mind off of what is going on." I almost get teary-eyed with my emotional self.

I pull up to the shop with the camera right behind me still rolling. The other Jones sisters might not want to be on camera but GG is down for it and she is awesome on film. She always got something funny to say. She is a natural and actually takes the attention off of me, which is great. I am finishing this season but by no means am I happy about it.

"They are going to film us getting our hair done? Why wouldn't they just wait 'til we got done?"

"GG, you look good no matter what." I slide out of the car and throw on a happy face. I am still not pleased that the producers wouldn't cancel the rest of the season, but so be it.

"Honey, look at you just a glowing. You are so gorge," Myron, my beautician, greets me at the door holding it open for GG and me. His red pouty lips match his red leather pants and the red lips on his metallic see-through blouse. I glance at his footwear because I know they are going to give me everything. And as I expected, they do. His studded red bottoms are hot.

"Hey, babe." I smooch both of Myron's cheeks.

"Are you alright, honey? I can kick all these cameras out if you like," Myron whispers as we walk to the waiting area.

"It's okay," I say as I roll my eyes. "It's an occupational hazard having cameras and nosey people all in my face, even in my worst moments." I sit down in a comfy leather chair.

"You must be GG. Angel has told me so much about you." Myron turns his attention to GG and pulls her in for a hug. "Oh my goodness. Your beautiful silver tresses are giving me life." Myron pulls away examining GG's hair while GG stands speechless, eyes wide, wondering what in the world is going on.

"Angel, I thought you said your girlfriend Judie was going to do my hair." Her squinted eyes and turned up nose look over Myron's shoulder at me.

"No, no, GG." I can't help but to laugh and Myron doubles over laughing too along with everyone else in the room. "Judie is just a word used for a great male friend that is gay," I explain. "Myron is going to lay your hair out." I quickly stand up and walk over to her. "You alright with that?" I whisper in her ear. I never thought about the fact that GG might have a problem with a man doing her hair. The camera crew, Myron, and myself all wait for GG's response. I don't want her to feel uncomfortable.

"Well if you trust him on your hair, I am fine. I just never had a man do my hair."

GG takes Myron's hand and checks out his gel tip nails. I can physically see Myron take a deep exhale. I am sure he doesn't want any awkward moments on TV.

"Baby, I am sure Angel has told you I am Christian and an old school one at that but don't think I am gon' be some judgmental Bible thumper." GG continues talking to Myron as he leads her to a chair. "Sweetheart, we are all children of God and don't let nobody tell you different. God loves you just as he loves me."

I can see Myron's eyes watering. We have talked about God and he has expressed how some Christians, including his own family members, have condemned him to Hell because of his lifestyle. But like I told him how I was raised, *"Judge not lest ye be judged."* It is not my or anyone else's place or ability to condemn anyone to Hell.

"Thank you," Myron whispers and GG pats his hand.

I grab a tissue out of my purse to wipe the tears from my eyes. You can never tell what a person is dealing with and how a few words can lift them up and encourage them, and I think that is just what GG did for Myron. I dig into my purse and pull out my mail. The first envelope I see doesn't have a return address and it has a Colombian stamp on it. My heart starts racing. I know it must be from Alejandro. I clumsily unfold the letter, intrigued but also scared of what he has written. My hands tremble as I closely hold the one-page letter to my face, making sure to keep it out of the view of cameras. I look up to see the camera focused on GG and Myron who are talking and laughing like they have known each other forever. Convinced that no one is paying me any attention, I look back at the letter.

Mija,

I hope this letter finds you doing well. There is still so much I need to tell you. A letter is not the way it should be told but there are a few things I want you to know. Angel, I never disowned you or asked or forced your mother to. When I found out you were not my child, yes, it hurt me. It broke my heart, but I was also relieved when your mother said she wanted you to move with your father's mother so you would have a chance at a normal life. The only thing I have ever wanted for you was for you to be happy and be able to have a good life, and I knew growing up in Colombia around me and the life I lead would prevent that.

And now I see that you leaving Colombia was the best thing for you. I am so proud of the woman you have grown to be; beautiful, intelligent, and most importantly, strong. I love you, Angel, and will always be there for you whenever you need me.

Tanga una vida bonita

Have a beautiful life...

I notice the letter being soaked by my tears and quickly wipe my eyes. Myron has GG under the dryer and comes for me.

"You and GG are getting on well." I smile at Myron as we walk back to the sinks.

"She's an angel." Myron's gap-toothed smile peeks from between his red lips.

"I know," I choke up, feeling overwhelmed with the thought of how blessed I am to have this life and to have my GG. Yes, my name is Angel but she is definitely the angel of my life. Alejandro is absolutely right; there is no telling how my life would have turned out if I never left Colombia. Who would I be if I had been raised by the selfish narcissist that birthed me?

"Come on, Angel." Myron lightly taps my shoulder when he is finished washing my hair.

Sitting under the dryer next to GG, I can't help thinking about Daniel. I miss my husband but I don't know what to do.

God, did I make the wrong choice in choosing Daniel or is this just me reaping what I sowed? Why try to do right when everything in my life keeps going wrong? I feel like no matter how I've tried to change I am falling into some of the same traps as my sisters. What a vicious cycle my family is trapped in. *Destroy the yoke*. The words float into my head. I remember hearing sermons about that when I was younger and GG talks about it a lot too. She taught us how sometimes people have to pay for the sins of their father. But Beau, Bella, and I have been determined to break the pattern of broken women and fatherless kids. I really did think Daniel was the love of my life.

"Baby, what's wrong?" GG grabs my hand. She can read the concern written on my face

"I-I-I…Daniel. GG, I don't know."

I want to tell GG. I know she will have some words of wisdom but I feel like saying it out loud makes our problems more real.

"What, baby? What about Daniel?"

"We got married but—"

"That is so good, baby."

"But GG, now with the Savannah baby mama drama I feel like we are falling apart," I whisper. "I've been hearing that her car has been at his house all day. I didn't do anything to deserve this. The truth of what she did is so out of the norm of course I got mad at him at first. Who would believe a man when they hear and see all that stuff?"

I look around and notice Evan chatting it up with Myron and Shannon and the camera guys outside having a smoke.

"That's the problem, baby. You didn't believe in him. Where was your faith when all that mess went on?"

"Now faith is the substance of things hoped for, the evidence of things not seen," we say in unison, reciting Hebrew 11:1, a scripture about faith.

"What do you mean, GG? I have faith in God, pray to God, and believe in God, but look where I am. Pregnant and alone." I notice my voice rising in frustration and then

213

quickly quiet it down.

"Baby, how many times have I told you that the word of God is to be applied to all aspects of life, not just your relationship with God? Where was your faith in your husband when you heard the news about the baby? You automatically believed the worst-case scenario and went off on him. You didn't take the time to listen to him. You had no faith in your husband. From what you have told me and what I have seen of the young man when I met him, he seems like a good man."

"I didn't even think about that." GG's words are like a light bulb going on in my mind. She is right.

"You want to keep your man?"

"Yes, ma'am. I love him so much."

"Then you better go save your marriage."

"But—"

"Now." GG gives me a one liner and I know exactly what she means. It is now or never. If I want to save my marriage and have any chance at being happy I have to see Daniel now before Savannah digs her nails in and tries to steal my man. I know she got pregnant in hopes of getting back with him.

"But I am set to film for the next few hours. I am supposed to hang out with Kylie and Tori tonight."

"Girl, you been trying to avoid the cameras since I been in town. Don't play yourself." GG laughs at her usage of current slang.

"Aw, GG, you throwing shade." I say, laughing with her.

"Look, you can just drop me off at home and tell them you are getting ready for later. Sneak out in your car and go save your marriage," GG quickly tells me the plan she's thought of.

"GG, you made up a lie?" I cut my eyes at her.

"I'm not lying. I'm simply making a suggestion. You are the one that's gon' be lying. GG will pray for you."

She winks her eye.

* * * * *

After we are finished getting our hair done, I put GG's plan into action. I pull into the garage, park the Maserati, hop into my black Range Rover, and quickly whip out, contemplating how I will approach Daniel. *Baby, I missed you. Let's never fight again.* Nah, too cheesy. *Daniel, we need to talk.* No, that sounds too serious.

I decide not to call him and just pop up at his house—no, our house. I feel my fresh blown out hair sticking to the back of my neck. I am so nervous I am sweating in the cool Atlanta air. "I can do this. I can do this," I give myself a pep talk as I pull up right in front of the house. I get out and pause when I see the pearl white Mercedes-Benz with tags that read SAVANNAH still parked at the house. I feel sick to my stomach and lean on to my truck to catch myself from falling. The sun starts to quickly fade away behind some clouds as I look up and start praying. "I love him, God. I can't lose him but I don't know." A crackle of lightening sparks up the grey sky and the thunder cracks through my thoughts. As the rain begins to lightly drop I consider my options. I can get in my car, leave, and admit defeat, or I can go get my man.

"I am getting my man."

I head towards the door as the rain starts pouring down. I ignore the bright headlights pulling up in the long driveway. Fist balled up, I beat on the door with all my might and I feel a slight throb as pain shoots through my hand. Waiting feels like an eternity as I continue to knock. I have a key. I don't know why I don't just use it. I stop banging on the door and begin fiddling for the key on my key ring.

"Angel!" I hear Evan's voice from behind me. Startled, I drop my keys and Evan stops talking. I know the cameras are probably on and rolling but I no longer care. They want a show, I am going to give them one.

I start beating on the door with my left hand and aggressively push the doorbell with my right. What is going on in this house? I am freaking out.

"Angel?" A stunned Daniel finally opens the door. I don't say anything or wait for him to say anything else. Standing on my tippy-toes, I wrap my hands around his neck and lean into his lips. Eyes closed, I just let my lips melt into his. I can't let go until I feel him, until I feel something, until I know he feels how much I love him. I have waited my whole life to have a man that I am sure will never leave and abandon me and he is it. Daniel's arms finally embrace me. He pulls me close to him and rubs my back.

"I love you." As tears run down my face I pull away to look into Daniel's eyes.

"I love you." I am so happy to hear the words from his mouth.

"I am so sorry that I didn't have faith in you and that I didn't listen to you. I know…" I almost repeat GG's words verbatim they ring so true. But I also feel like I need to tell him why I react the way I do when we have problems. All my life I have felt like the men that were supposed to be there for me left me and forgot about me like I wasn't enough for them to love. The man I had always thought was my father I was made to believe didn't want me. My real father was dead and gone before I ever knew about him. As for every man I have dated, none of them stuck around

216

long enough to really get to know me because they were so focused on sex.

"I…I…" I stutter as I try to start explaining things to Daniel. Then I notice Savannah standing right behind us looking annoyed with a crying David in her arms.

"Oh my gosh, I had just got him to sleep and here you come beating down the door. Uh, how—?"

"Oh, he is so adorable," I cut her off. "Can I hold him?"

"No!" Savannah protests.

"Yes, of course." Daniel takes David out of Savannah's hands and places him into mine.

"He's perfect." I stand in the doorway looking into David's bright hazel eyes that look just like Daniel's. His little fat cheeks and deep dimples are perfect. I take a deep whiff of him. Yes, I am a baby smeller and he smells so good. His blue little pajamas look like he is here for the night.

"Buenos noches, David. Yo soy Angel, tu madrastra." I am in love with him already and by the way he has stopped crying and started cooing I think the feeling is mutual.

I hum a Spanish lullaby as I rock David in my arms, oblivious to anything else going on around me.

"Give me my baby!" Savannah snatches David out of my arms and he immediately starts to cry again.

"What is wrong with you?" Daniel glares at Savannah, obviously upset that she snatched David out of my arms.

"No, I don't know her. I don't know if I want my son around her, Daniel," Savannah argues. I wonder if there is any validity to her argument. She doesn't know me but I am married to her son's father. And honestly, based on how David was conceived she needs to tread lightly with what she says about me.

"She is my wife and—"

"It's okay," I cut Daniel off. "Let's go in the house. I know there is a lot for us to discuss."

"Your wife?" Savannah and Evan both blurt out. I had forgotten that he and the camera crew were even here. I am sure Evan is loving the show.

"I don't care who she is. I don't want her around my baby. I am leaving." Savannah walks into the house, I assume to get her purse and David's things.

"That's fine but David is staying." Daniel follows behind Savannah and I'm behind him and Evan with the camera crew is behind me.

"Not if she is staying." Savannah stomps around the living room, picking up her purse and an expensive Gucci diaper bag.

"He is my son and she is my wife. You are going to have to deal." Daniel's voice is calm and matter-of-fact. Just hearing him call me his wife over and over again makes me feel good.

I know we have a long way to go with my personal issues and Savannah's issues, but having him standing beside me defending me makes me feel like everything will be okay.

Savannah's face is as red as her hair as she continues to scream at Daniel. She is shouting out things about court, her having full custody and supervised visitation, and I finally get fed up.

"Please stop acting like you are without fault. You impregnated yourself with frozen semen from a man you haven't been with in over a year. Do you really think taking Daniel to court is going to be good for you?"

"You stupid bitch!" Savannah rushes towards me

screaming at the top of her lungs. Her fantasy of Daniel getting back with her is quickly fading away.

"David needs both his parents together raising him as a family. So why don't you go find you a basketball player or something and move the hell on?"

"Look, like it or not I am Daniel's wife and our family is rapidly growing. I am pregnant and David is going to be a big brother. Regardless of how I feel about you and what you did I love that baby."

I look at David still crying in Savannah's hands. Aside from his cries, the room is dead silent with all eyes on me. Daniel and I have just dropped two bombs within a five-minute period and no doubt everyone in the room is shocked.

Savannah charges towards me with rage in her eyes. "You're lying. She is lying, Daniel. Don't believe her. She's trying to say and do any and everything to keep—"

"Keep what?" Daniel sneers at Savannah with disgust. "Keep us apart?"

"Yes, don't you see?" Savannah pleas.

"We will never be together again. I have told you this more than once. You have to be delusional to think having David would change that."

"Aghhhhh!" Savannah shrieks. With David in one arm she takes her free hand and shoves Daniel in his chest as hard as she can. Daniel stumbles over an end table trying to avoid falling into me and there is a popping noise as his leg buckles and he falls to the ground.

"My ankle!" Daniel moans out in pain. He must have twisted it or something.

"I am calling an ambulance," Evan screams out with what I think is actual genuine concern and care for once. "Daniel, are you okay?"

219

"Call the police!" Daniel yells at Evan.

"No!" Savannah and I both scream out.

"Look at what she just did; what she is trying to do. She is trying to break us up. She is crazy, Angel!" Daniel yells from the ground and I see him grimacing with pain as he tries to stand up.

"She is David's mother. Come on, you can't send her to jail," I plead with Daniel. I will be the bigger woman; the woman God wants me to be.

"Give me my son and get out."

Daniel eases himself onto a chair as Savannah remains silent, looking at us. David hasn't stopped crying. All this commotion has him so cranky.

"No, Daniel, I am not leaving my baby," Savannah argues.

"Yes, you are. Either now or after the police get here. You attacked me for no reason. I don't want my son anywhere near you right now. You need help, Savannah."

Noooo!" Savannah cries out and darts for the door.

"Stay with him," I order Evan and I run towards the door, chasing Savannah. I can hear the ambulance already nearing the house. I have to make sure David is okay.

"Savannah!" I scream as I exit the house. She is standing on the porch still shaking, debating whether or not to run out into the pouring rain.

"You did this. Daniel will never see his son again!" Savannah looks back at me and screeches. I see the ambulance lights pulling into the large circular driveway. Savannah screams something inaudible as the sirens are blaring loudly.

"NOOOOOOOOOOOOOO!" I scream. The ambulance tires screech as thunder booms and lighting streaks through the sky.

"Oh my God!" I cry out as David whimpers.

Donisha Derice & Jai Darlene

19
Spotlight

Kylie

I'm sitting on a hard metal chair shivering in a freezing room, waiting and consumed with anger. The room is dim, however the ceiling light is hanging so low it's nearly hitting me on top of my head. Detective Robinson walks in and the light from outside the room is blinding. By instinct I attempt to shield my eyes.

"Ouch," I whisper to myself. I hurt my wrist trying to cover my eyes. I forgot my right arm is cuffed to the table.

"Is this really necessary?" I complain, referring to being chained liked an animal.

"You know it is," Detective Robinson responds without a hint of care in her voice.

"I promise you I will sue you for everything you have. You will be walking around in your period panties for the next ten years. This is police brutality!" I say through clenched teeth.

I can still hear the officer yelling at me when I got arrested.

"Put your hands in the air! Put your hands in the air, right now!" the officer growled at me. I quickly put my hands in the air. Then after Detective Robinson told me I was being arrested for murder, the male officer started yelling at me again.

"Get out of the vehicle!" I hesitated out of fear. "I said get out of the vehicle!" I began to lower my hands to pull the door handle.

"Put your hands in the air. I must see your hands at all

223

times!" the officer barked at me.

"How am I supposed to keep my hands in the air and get out of the car at the same time?" I asked, wanting the officer to clarify his stupidity.

Before I could blink my eyes a second officer swung my car door open and yanked me out the car. I hooked on to the officer's uniform to keep from falling flat on my face. Before I could get my bearings, the officer unnecessarily began yanking on my arm, trying to put my hands in cuffs. I was done being frightened and I became livid. I'd had enough of being manhandled when Logan was alive. I wasn't going to continue to be abused, so I full throttled my knee into the officer's crotch. The first officer hit me in the head with the butt of his gun and I put my hands in the air. I didn't want to fight a losing battle; I was just enraged about how I was being treated.

The second officer, clearly upset that I got the best of him, shoved me against my car, and that's when all hell broke loose. He swung me around as if he was going to slam me to the ground, but Detective Robinson intervened.

"Fall back, Officer Elliot! She's pregnant. We cannot afford any incidents!" Detective Robinson ordered.

"I'm tired of you entitled spoiled brats getting whatever you want whenever you want it," Officer Elliot whispered in my ear. I hope they give you the electric chair. Your daddy's money can't get you out of this."

He twisted my arm behind my back and it felt like it was going to be ripped out of its socket. I yelped in pain and he slapped me in the back of my head. I reached my free hand back and yanked his hair until I had a fistful of his hair plugs in my hand. I kicked and squirmed as the officers used full force to handcuff me.

"Stop it. Stop it right now, Kylie," I heard Detective

Robinson's voice say. "We want to take you in quietly without incident. No one knows you are being arrested."

After I was put in the back seat of the police car, I heard her ranting at Officer Elliot. "What the hell? That was not the plan."

Pulling me from my thoughts Detective Robinson addresses my claims of police brutality.

"If you didn't try to resist arrest you wouldn't be in this situation. In fact, if you didn't murder your husband you wouldn't be in this situation."

"I didn't murder anyone," I say with disgust. I already know the card she's playing. I can tell she intends to stick with her own. The blue is thicker than blood—my blood, which was all over the officers after they brutalized me. They've already come up with a story to make it look like the bruises they gave me were my own fault.

"Before you say anything else..." She slides a waiver and a pen across the table. "You have the right to remain silent. Anything you say or do can and will be used against you in a court of law. You have the right to an attorney. If you cannot afford an attorney, one will be appointed to you. If you understand your rights sign the waiver please."

I sign the waiver with my free hand. "I have nothing to hide. I already told you everything I know."

"Tell me, how did you kill Logan Beckham?"

"Mario Kessler killed Logan Beckham," I declare as Detective Robinson stares blankly at me. "Like I said before, Mario has been infatuated with me, borderline stalking me, with nonstop phone calls and showing up at our house. Did you check our phone records? Did you find my key fob he stole at his house?"

"We did. But explain to me if he stole your keys why you never changed your locks or called the police."

"Because I didn't know it was stolen. I thought I lost it at the gala. He showed up at my house uninvited minutes before I was scheduled to go to Miami for my show, and he confessed he stole them then. I provided you with the security tapes to prove that."

The security videos have no sound and only show the outside of the house and I gladly handed over all the videos to Detective Robinson. I have weeks of tapes showing Mario coming and going out of my house.

"Hmmm, interesting. He just showed up uninvited, huh?" Detective Robinson's tone is screaming with sarcasm. "Tell me again about the shooting? I want to make sure I have your story straight for when we go to trial."

"I came home and Mario and Logan were in the living room..." I pause and choose my words carefully. "...arguing."

Fired up, Detective Robinson says, "You hesitated again! You hesitated the first time you gave your statement and you are hesitating again. What are you hiding?"

There's no way I'm going to admit that I caught my husband giving another man fellatio.

"I'm sorry. This is just so hard for me." I start to sob. "I didn't know Mario's infatuation would turn into this. I thought it was just a cute little crush. I was flattered," I say as tears roll down my face. "My husband was annoyed, but I was flattered. Neither one of us thought he was dangerous. He was a family friend."

In a soft tone, trying to play good cop, Detective Robinson says. "So they were arguing. Continue."

I try speaking through my sobs.

"I heard arguing in the living room. This was strange to me, because I recognized the voices but I didn't see Mario's car parked outside. So I went to the living room to see what was going on. Mario saw me and tried to run over to greet me, but Logan yanked him back by his arm. Mario began to confess his undying love for me. Maybe I'm a ditz or something, because I took it as a joke. I laughed. I told him he did realize he was professing his love in front of my husband, who is the only man I will ever love. Mario pulled out his gun and pointed at it me. Then I don't know what happened. It all happened so fast. All I know is all three of us tussled for the gun. I almost fell to the ground and I clutched the couch to keep from falling. I looked over into Mario's menacing eyes that said *if I can't have you no one can* and the next thing I know the gun exploded. I saw a white flash and I stood there in a daze. I felt like the whole room was whirling. Once I came to my senses, I realized Logan was on floor unconscious with his blood spilling on the white rug from a hole in his chest. I rushed to his side and cradled his head in my lap and dialed 911. When the operator asked me who shot my husband, I told her it was Mario, who was nowhere in sight.

"Hmph. Let me tell you the evidence I have against you and why I'm not buying your little story. We found Mario's keys at your house and the video surveillance shows Mario coming and leaving out of your house several times. Your neighbor, Jordyn, tells us she saw Mario's car parked in the neighborhood on several occasions. Mario was constantly calling your house when your husband was scheduled for games. Skylar Jennings is willing to testify against you that she heard you guys arguing in your hotel room in Miami. What was that argument about? Your affair? All the evidence, everything you have told me, leads me to believe you were actually having an affair. Now you are trying to turn the tables and make it look like Mario was crazy and stalking you."

"He was!" I defend myself. She has to believe me. I can't go to prison. I have to hustle myself out of this murder charge.

"No, no. You were having an affair and I have the ultimate trump card that will prove it." Detective Robinson nods towards my stomach.

I look down at my growing belly and rub it.

"You mean this is your proof?"

She nods her head.

"Mario told me everything. He told me you were having an affair and that the baby you are carrying is his. He told me how you plotted to kill Logan because you weren't happy in your marriage and you wanted to start a new life with him. It was Mario that tried to stop you from killing Logan."

That motherfu...this is some bull. They are trying to take all the evidence I provided them and use it against me. I'm not going to let that happen. I sit up straight in my chair and look Detective Robinson in the eyes with a straight face.

"My truth is all the evidence I need."

Donisha Derice & Jai Darlene

The Reunion Show

"I didn't miss anything, did I?" Deliscia asks as she struts into the living room holding a bottle of wine and a bowl of popcorn. Kay and Jessica sit on the couch, eyes already glued to the screen watching a recap of the latest season of *Sports Wives*, their favorite ratchet reality show.

"Turn it up!" Jessica reaches for the remote control. Kay snatches the bowl of popcorn from Deliscia without looking her way.

"So what y'all think? Did Kylie do it?" Deliscia sits on the couch in between her two besties. She has been waiting all week to get answers, hoping that the reunion host Cindy Wilson doesn't hold any punches and gets right into the drama.

"Girl, shhhh. We about to find out," Jessica says, shrugging her shoulders.

"Ladies and gents, it's the moment you all have been waiting for! We somehow managed to get all the ladies from the cast of *Sports Wives* on this stage," Cindy announces with a huge grin across her face. Her long blonde wig is flowing down her back and her big boobs ooze over in her wrap dress. Her long legs strut to her chair in the center of the stage.

"Oh yeah, it's about to go down," Jessica says in a singsong voice.

"The Rose is here," she says, imitating Kylie's voice.

Look at Skylar's punk butt. I hope someone slaps that smug smile off her face," Kay says, rolling her eyes as the camera pans over the stage, getting a close up of each of the wives one by one.

"I'm surprised they ain't filming Kylie from jail in an orange jumpsuit. I know she murdered her husband,"

Deliscia remarks. Jessica cuts her eyes at Deliscia.

"Naw, she's too fabulous for that. Look at those stilettos. I need a pair," Kay points out Kylie's shoes.

"Yeah, I'm with Kay. It doesn't make sense," Jessica argues. "Why would she kill her husband? They are young, fly, and rich."

"Y'all always ganging up on me," Deliscia pouts.

"All you ladies look so fabulous. And Kylie, I'm so glad you are not rocking an orange jumpsuit," Cindy giggles. "But you would make it look good."

"See, see. I told y'all. Me and Cindy on the same level!" Deliscia beams with excitement.

"Yeah, I bet some people would love to see that," Kylie laughs. "But here I am looking like vindication. All those false allegations against me have been dropped."

Kay laughs.

"Okay, Kylie on the stage flowing, sounding like Tupac."

The camera shoots over to Jordyn who is scoffing and rolling her eyes to the back of her head.

"Yeah, right. I don't know what you said to get out of it, but I know you are guilty," she hisses.

"You don't know anything. You are guilty of being boring, which is why you are making up all these lies to get camera time," Angel scoffs at Jordyn.

"Whoa, ladies, let's calm down a little bit. I want to hear what Jordyn has to say," Cindy intervenes.

"Cindy, I saw everything. Kylie and I are neighbors and I saw Mario's car in our neighborhood on several occasions, including the day of Logan's murder. She was having an affair with him and I promptly told the police, which is why they issued a warrant for her arrest."

Jordyn's accusations make Kylie laugh, but Jordyn

continues to talk over Kylie.

"Let's talk facts. Her fingerprints were on the gun. She is pregnant with Mario's love child, so she killed Logan when he found out about her scandalous ass."

"You can't be serious," Kylie laughs. "You want to talk facts? Let's talk facts. Fact, I'm carrying my husband's child." Kylie rubs her belly. "After your fictitious allegations the police required me to get a pregnancy DNA test that proved Logan is the father of my child. Fact, my fingerprints were on the gun because Logan and I tried to get the gun away from Mario. Fact, Mario had become obsessed with me and tried to shoot me and my husband lost his life trying to protect me. Fact, Mario's fingerprint was on the trigger and not mine. Fact, I am not guilty of my husband's murder and I cannot by any means take you or anybody else seriously who thinks I am," Kylie calmly states, knowing the real truth.

That night went exactly how she planned. Lying to Logan about carrying Mario's child, Kylie knew it would set him off. Had Kylie not deleted the video recording on her phone from that night the whole world would know about her dirty deed, which is why she was in a panic to erase it.

During the struggle with the gun Kylie's stiletto heel got tangled in the white fur rug and she fell. Logan and Mario continued to struggle. It only took a few seconds for Mario to take control of the gun, but Logan grabbed the barrel, fighting to get it back. Kylie watched, hoping they would accidentally kill each other. Instead of waiting for fate to intervene, she quickly got up and forced Mario's finger on the trigger and pulled it. *BANG!* The explosion filled the room and blood started leaking from Logan's chest. Technically speaking, Kylie had done it. She forced

Mario's hand to pull the trigger. Kylie watched as Logan struggled to breathe and took that moment to tell him the truth.

"I want to be free and I'll never be free with you alive," she whispered to him. Logan spurted, struggling to say something.

"Shut up!" Kylie harshly said as she ruthlessly slapped Logan's face. "You've said everything you are ever going to say!" In a softer tone, she said, "I thought the post-nup would protect me, but I don't trust you. As long as you're alive you will always be able to hold my secrets against me." Kylie paused, contemplating pushing and twisting her finger into his bullet hole to make blood gush from his chest in excruciating pain, but she decided against it. "Besides, this is payback for every time you have slapped, punched, pushed, and kicked me."

Kylie stroked his face. "I loved you. I really did, before you started beating me, even for a time afterwards. But you destroyed me and I have to do the same to you. I owe it to you and I always pay my debts."

Kylie looked up to see Mario frozen in shock as the gun slipped from his fingers dropping to the floor.

"That's yours," she said, looking down at the gun. "You better take it and run. I'm going to call the police and tell them what *you* did."

Frantic and not knowing what to do, Mario did as Kylie ordered. He grabbed the gun and ran out of the Beckham home.

I Frank Underwooded Mario, the police department, and the world, for that matter, Kylie thinks to herself as she sits back into the couch and continues to smile at the fact that she has learned how to master getting everyone to do and believe exactly what she wants.

"Well tell them how it really is!" Cindy's pursed lips glisten with her red lipstick. "We are going to take a short commercial break and when we get back we'll talk to the other pregnant wife whose season was filled with her own drama."

The camera focuses in on Angel who is whispering to Kylie.

"Whatever. That bitch is lying," Deliscia says. "She did it."

She takes a sip of her wine.

"I want to see these so-called DNA results."

"Cold hearted. She is pregnant and left with a toddler too. Where is your sympathy? The police would have never dropped the charges if they actually had evidence proving she did it," Jessica says, sticking up for Kylie.

"Plus, Kylie is about her business. She has single-handedly revamped her company's whole branding image. Do you really think she would ruin all she is working for? Anyway, what reason did she have to kill Logan in the first place?" Kay chimes in before stuffing her mouth with some popcorn.

"Because she got caught having an affair. Duh!" Deliscia rolls her eyes at Jessica and Kay.

"And you got this information from who? Jordyn's ol' boring no-storyline-having self? Like Angel said, she was just trying to stay relevant on the show," Jessica argues, sounding like Kylie's criminal defense attorney.

"Okay, okay. The show is back on. I want to hear what really went down between Angel, Savannah, and Daniel."

Kay turns the TV up over Jessica and Deliscia, who are still arguing about Kylie's guilt or innocence.

"Okay and we are back!" Cindy has a devious grin on her face. "One of my favorite storylines was the fairytale romance between Daniel and Angel Silver. Let's take a look back at their love and basketball over the season."

Videos of Angel and Daniel start to play on the television screen, starting with his proposal and ending with the fight with Savannah.

"And now, joining us on stage are Daniel and Savannah!" Cindy, the audience, and a couple of the wives clap.

"Okay, so the season started off with you two sharing all your love in the spotlight but things quickly got secretive, including a very private marriage and an even more hidden pregnancy. Or should I say pregnancies?" Cindy gives Angel and Daniel the side eye as Angel sits holding Daniel's hand.

"I wouldn't necessarily say secretive. Those who needed to know knew," Angel giggles, rolling her eyes.

"So Kylie, did you know about the marriage or the baby? Girl, spill the tea. I mean you two are supposed to be sisters." Cindy uses air quotes when saying *sisters*.

"Of course I knew about my sister's pregnancy and marriage," Kylie lies, her lips dripping with sarcasm.

"Yeah, they sisters alright. Sister hoes just like *Sister Wives*," Skylar chimes in, laughing at her own joke.

"Speaking of *Sister Wives...*" Cindy frowns up her face shaking her head at Skylar. "The whole scenario with Angel and Savannah could definitely be a TV reel for *Sister Wives* gone wrong. Let's talk a little about Daniel and his babies' mamas' drama."

"First off, Cindy, I am his wife, not his baby's mama." Angel holds out her hand with her ten karats shining on camera.

That's right, Angel! Show 'em!" Jessica screams. "I hate when people do that, trying to relegate every woman to baby mama status. The rock on her hand says differently."

She sips her wine in disgust.

"That's right, baby," Daniel cosigns for his wife.

"And Savannah is a baby mama by deceit," Kylie says, giving Savannah the evil eye.

"Yes, honey, let's jump right into that." Cindy sits up in her chair, obviously excited about this subject. "So can you explain exactly how David's cutie pie self came to be?"

"No, Cindy. I will not be discussing that. I am currently going through court proceedings in regards to my son." Savannah shakes her head.

"What she on the show for? She's there to talk. Talk, hoe. We already know what your THOT ass did!" Deliscia yells at the TV screen, throwing popcorn at it.

"Yeah, Savannah, I think you are trying to take the easy way out. You know everybody wants to know how it happened." Cindy rolls her eyes and flips her hair.

"Well, Cindy, I don't know the specifics, like if she used a turkey baster or what, but David was conceived by semen that Savannah stole from my husband."

Angel turns her nose up in disgust.

"So Daniel, you are saying you did not have sex with Savannah and that is not how David was conceived?" Cindy inquires.

"That is exactly what I am saying, Cindy. Savannah and I had been long broken up when she got pregnant and I found out the same time the rest of the world did," Daniel scoffs.

"Well ya' daddy obviously knew. We were told that not only did he supply DNA for the test, but he also paid for it, and was right at Savannah's side when she came forward with the results." Cindy's eyes buck wide as she waits for an answer.

"That is because Dennis has always supported Daniel's and my relationship and was hoping that the birth of his first grandchild would bring us back together." Savannah leans forward in her chair to get a good view of Angel.

"Oh, okay." Cindy starts eating air popcorn and sits back like she's at the movies waiting for a response.

"Yeah, Savannah is right. My dad would love for me to marry a certain type of woman and I guess Savannah fits that type," Daniel says, making a subtle reference to the fact that his father did not want him to marry a black woman. "But thank goodness I am my own man and chose to marry the woman I love."

"So how has David's surprise birth affected you and Daniel's relationship?" Cindy probes, still eating her air popcorn.

"I mean we are so happy and blessed to have David in our lives he has brought Daniel and I closer together," Angel beams.

"Yeah, closer together like when he had to come to the hospital when you passed out over hearing about Daniel being that baby's daddy." Skylar rolls her eyes as she, Jordyn, and Elle burst out laughing.

"Right. Angel, we heard about all the MF'ers and bastards Daniel was when you first found out. And it was all on social media and gossip blogs when Savannah was at Daniel's all night long the same day you got released from the hospital." Cindy sits under a shady palm tree in a breeze with the shade she just threw at Angel.

"Right!" Savannah echoes in. "As you saw from the footage, I was at Daniel's house with our son enjoying a lovely evening when she barged in like the ghetto girlfriend from hell."

"Now you got something to say," Cindy laughs.

"Yes, I do. Angel attacked me that night, almost killed me, and now she is trying to take my son away from me." Savannah fake cries and Skylar hands her a tissue.

"Okay, you are talking about the infamous missing footage. The cameras were inside with Daniel, who you shoved, breaking his ankle. But what happened outside of Daniel's mansion that night?" Cindy inquires.

"Angel!" Savannah screams.

"Wow, calm down and hold that thought. We will be right back."

Cindy stands up clapping her hands, encouraging the audience to clap too.

"I need to use the restroom," Angel says, standing up slowly, with one hand using the couch as leverage and the other holding her baby bump.

"Me too."

Kylie stands up next to Angel and they walk off stage.

"You know, you never told me what happened that night," Kylie whispers once they are in the bathroom.

Angel hadn't told anybody the truth. It would stay between her, God, and Savannah, who no one will believe. When Savannah ran outside into the rain, Angel had followed closely behind her, screaming about her not taking David.

"You are not taking him. You are crazy!" Angel screamed, grabbing Savannah's arm.

"You will never be around my son or really have Daniel!" Savannah had yelled while trying to pull away from the tight grip Angel had on her arm. "You are not made for this life so why don't you go back to the 'hood, or better yet, go find a basketball player like your sister did.

238

Isn't that how all you black girls roll?" Savannah continued to insult Angel.

Then, it happened so quickly, Angel didn't realize what she had really done. As Savannah continued to try and pull away, Angel placed her foot on the step right in front of Savannah, and took David out of her arm. When Angel let Savannah's arm go, she watched as Savannah tripped and fell hard onto the cobblestone driveway just as the ambulance screeched to a stop, barely missing running her over.

"Girl, her crazy butt went running into the rain and fell. Thank goodness I was there to catch David and if that ambulance hadn't stopped in time she would have been a goner. And that is why we have temporary custody and are fighting for sole custody," Angel quickly rehearses the lie she going to tell when she is back on stage.

"Are you ladies ready?" Evan asks, tapping on the door.

"Almost," Angel and Kylie yell in unison before using the restroom.

Back on the stage Savannah looks poised to tell the world what Angel had done. *Daniel will hate her for this. She tried to hurt me while I was holding David. He is definitely going to leave her and then we will be one big happy family.* Savannah smiles to herself.

"Okay, and we are back. Now Savannah, you have something to say about that night?" The camera pans from Cindy over to Savannah.

"Yes. Angel tried to kill me! She intentionally tripped me as the ambulance was pulling up!" Savannah's face turns red as she tries to tell her truth about that night.

"Yeah right," Daniel laughs. "Your inability to tell the truth is one of the many reasons I could never see myself

239

being with you. Angel is a better mother to David then you can ever be."

"You ran outside in the rain in a pair of heels while carrying a newborn baby and you want to blame me. Own your dirt. What you did was stupid and reckless and that is why we have custody of David." Angel raises her voice, leaning up in the couch.

"Lies. Lies! You tried to kill me, bitch!" Savannah jumps up off the couch she is sitting on, running straight towards Angel with fire in her eyes. Her hand lunges at Angel but is quickly grabbed by Daniel. Her foot stomps on his bandaged bruised ankle and he releases her hand as he moans in pain. Security quickly swoops in and drags Savannah off the stage.

"Okay. We at RTV do not condone any violence and Savannah is being removed from the show. Let's take another brief break and come back and move onto Skylar's rocky relationships and many battles during the season." Cindy quickly goes over to Angel and Daniel to make sure they are okay.

"I think we are going to be fine." Angel gives a little smile. *Savannah has brought on her own demise. There is no way she will win the custody battle now*, Angel thinks to herself while shaking her head.

"Yeah right. They don't condone violence, but they sure did play out this fight scene," Jessica laughs.

The show comes back from break. "There was a very clear line dividing you ladies. Kylie, Angel, and Tori on one side, and Skylar, Elle, and Jordyn on the other. However, Skylar, it seems that when it came to drama this season, you were the center of it," Cindy remarks. A video montage starts playing, showing every single argument that Skylar had throughout the season, ending with a clip of

Kylie saying "Team Rich Bitch vs. Team Skank." The studio audience laughs at Kylie's remark on the video and a camera zooms in on Skylar squirming in her chair.

"There is no denying that Skylar and Kylie didn't get along, but why?" Cindy asks with a quizzical voice.

"Yes, Skylar, please tell everyone why you thought it was okay to attack a pregnant woman. I haven't done anything to you."

Skylar contemplates all the flack she has been given for attacking Kylie on the show and she decides to apologize to get back into the fans' good graces. "You know what? You have done things to me, but that doesn't excuse my behavior. I take responsibility for what I did and I shouldn't have come for you like that."

"Kylie, do you accept her apology?" Cindy asks.

"No, I don't accept that backhanded apology." Kylie frowns.

Skylar dismissively shrugs her shoulders. "I did what I could do and I'm done. My issues were never with her, they were was with Angel, but yet she kept sticking her nose in the middle and it got slapped. What do you want me to say?"

"She probably wants you to say sorry and mean it," Cindy quips

"Whatever, Cindy. Don't go there." Skylar flips her hand at Cindy. The crowd boos.

"I'm just telling the truth. You just admitted you had no reason to attack her, but yet you did and that apology you gave was sorry."

"I apologized and either she will accept it or not."

"Since you don't want to take responsibility for yourself, let's move on. Not only did you create drama for yourself, you instigated drama with everyone else. You accused Angel of having an affair with Elle's fiancé. I don't know if I believe you."

"You should. I know what I saw. She was all over him," Skylar accuses.

"Angel, just admit it. You spent the whole season avoiding me just so we couldn't discuss you trying to get with my man," Elle chimes in.

"I was too busy filming a movie. I don't have time for you or your drama. I told you what happened at the gala. I'm not going to keep explaining myself. It smells like you have on the fragrance he bought you," Angel says, turning her nose up. "And by the way, in case you haven't noticed, I am in a happy, loving relationship with the love of my life and have no desire to cheat. I'll leave that to Team Skank."

"Please, you are no better than your man-stealing, conniving sister!" Skylar retorts, rolling her eyes at Angel.

Cindy stands up, tugging her snug wrap dress.

"Okay, guys, we have to pay the bills. After the break we'll discuss how Tori swooped in on Skylar's man. Oh, by the way, Blake is here."

Cindy grins, dragging the word *here* out as the audience cheers. The screen fades out to a commercial.

"Oh shoot. It's going down," Deliscia says.

"I'm so Team Rich. That's what Skylar gets. She deserved to be dumped," Jessica remarks, and Deliscia and Kay nod their heads in agreement.

"Tori was kind of hoe-ish to sleep with him like that," Kay says. Deliscia and Jessica turn and give her death stares.

"But all's fair in love and sex," she says in an unsure voice.

The camera pans over the studio audience before zooming in on a smiling Cindy and her cleavage.

"Okay, back to discussing man-stealing, cheating skanks. Let's talk about how Blake went from Team Skylar to Team Tori."

"Hold on, Cindy. Who's the skank you are referring to? Skylar?" Kylie throws her head back, laughing.

"Whatever. The only skank in this room is Tori," Skylar quips.

"Ouch," Cindy says, making a pretend hurt face. "Do you say that because she took your man?"

"Cindy, I had just broken up with Blake and she had sex with him. Come on."

"Well, let's get Blake's side of the story."

Cindy grins and Blake walks out the stage and sits behind Tori.

"Umph, welcome Blake. You are one fine specimen," Cindy drools.

"Thank you, Cindy," Blake chuckles like he's used to the attention.

"So let's get straight to the point. Why did you dump Skylar and hours later you hooked up with Tori?"

"I didn't just hook up with Tori. I fell in love. I don't have to worry about being manipulated or lied to with Tori. She's authentic, the real deal. And you can't put a time frame on love."

"Whatever. Love my ass. You humiliate me on national TV and you want to call it love. You said you love me too. You'll be back."

"Oh, I didn't know your legs were back open for business, but Blake is mine now. Get over it," Tori says and Skylar lunges for her, but before she can get to Tori, security scoops Skylar up, lifting her off the floor and carrying her backstage kicking and screaming.

"Are you okay?" Cindy asks Tori and she nods her

head.

"Well that concludes this reunion special, but before we go, ladies, tell us what is next for you."

The camera pans over the stage and zooms in on Kylie.

"Well as you know, I'm the creative director of Rose and Company's marketing division. I'm doing my best with trying to transition to being a single working mom and it's not easy," Kylie says as Angel rubs her hand. "But I'm lucky I have a wonderful support system and I want to help other single moms so I started a college scholarship that will give full rides to single working mothers like myself that are trying to start their lives over." Everyone applauds and the camera pans to Angel.

"I'm currently promoting my movie *Money, Cash, Models*, which will be in theaters soon and I just landed the lead in a new movie which has graciously agreed to schedule filming around my pregnancy," Angel says with pride.

The camera pans to Tori.

"I'm currently working on a shoe line and building a strong foundation with Blake." Tori smiles and the camera pans to Elle.

"Isaque and I have finally set a wedding date for next fall, so I'm planning a wedding!" Elle exclaims, clasping her hands together with glee.

"And I—" Jordyn begins to talk but the closing music comes on and the camera pans to Cindy.

"Well that's it for this very compelling rollercoaster we call *Sport's Wives*. It's so real it's unscripted. Thank you all for tuning in and we hope to see you again next season!"

END SCENE

Donisha Derice's
Acknowledgements

Wow! Everything about this is such a blessing. I went years and years and years wanting to write and within one year I am having my second book published. My favorite scripture Jeremiah 29:11 says, "For I know the thoughts I think toward you, saith the Lord, thoughts of peace and not of evil, to give you an expected end." Although this is just the beginning of my writing career, I find peace in knowing where this is leading me. That feeling when you finally figure out what you want to do with your life and know it is exactly what you are supposed to be doing is indescribable. I love, love, love writing. It is allowing me to share stories with the world and I am looking forwarding to doing just that.

I want to thank all of my family and friends that continue to support me. When chasing dreams it is always good to have people there for you rooting you on. Specifically, I want to shout out Aunt Tiya, because you said I was going to get a whooping if I didn't. No, for real, you have always been down for your niece and supported me even when you fuss at me unnecessarily. Please believe that with some of the proceeds of this book I am going to get you a bottle of Remy Martin.

To my three critics, Mena, Sungano, and Jay that are always the first to read my work and always keep it real, thank you so much.

To my co-author and very, very, very dear friend Jai Darlene, as I have said before and will say forever, without you there would be no *Hustle: A Means to an End* or *Hustle: Unscripted.* God brought us together for this and I look forward to the journey our writings are taking us on. As we continue to write story after story I am so excited about our future. I know all our dreams will come true even without me getting with Richy Dollaz (LOL).

Last but definitely not least, to every person that loves a good story, here you go. *Unscripted* was so much fun to write. I lead a pretty normal life but do enjoy indulging in some ratchet reality TV and so I decided to write some. *Unscripted* is a fiction story that to me is one of a kind. This book gets deep into the real lives of reality TV stars, showing they are flawed and vulnerable just like everyone else. I really hope you enjoy this book and please keep a look out because there are so many more stories I want to share.

My writing will take me places and I look forward to you all taking the ride with me.

Jai Darlene's
Acknowledgements

The outpour of support we have received from friends, family, and fans of our work is overwhelming and I am more than grateful. Artists always think their work is good, but never know how it will be received by the public and I thank you for all the positive and constructive feedback received.

Thank you to all the libraries and bookstores who have stocked our book. Thanks to all the amazing book clubs, book fairs, and bloggers who gave us amazing reviews and interviews. Without you it would have been a million times harder to get our work out to the masses.

Thank you to Mena and Jay for being our ever-so-willing test subjects.

Thank you to my husband that goes over and beyond in keeping me encouraged. I don't know what Donisha and I would have done without your help and support with getting our work out there.

Thank you to Donisha, my day ten, my Kenya to my Cynthia, my platonic side piece lol. I literally could not have done all of this without you.

The fear of the Lord is the instruction of wisdom, and before honor is humility. (Proverbs 15:33) I humble myself in the presence of His Majesty. Lord, lift me to the place of highest honor as I continue to plant seeds of your wisdom in my work. Father, I know my work is a gift from you and I thank you for your blessings and grace.

Donisha Derice

Donisha Derice was born and raised in Indianapolis, IN, where she only dreamed of being two things: a lawyer and a writer. Receiving degrees in Paralegal Studies, Criminal Justice, and Public Management, she has worked for a legal agency for over 6 years, currently as an office project manager. After realizing she no longer desired to become an attorney, Donisha decided to follow her other dream. Her first novel, The Hustle, was completed while Donisha's plate was full with motherhood, college, and her full-time job. Donisha knows she has found her true passion and calling—and it is in writing.

Connect with Donisha:
www.jaianddonisha.com
www.facebook.com/jaianddonisha
www.twitter.com/donishaderice
www.instagram.com/donishaderice

Jai Darlene

Jai Darlene is an army brat who traveled all over the world with her family before settling down in Fort Wayne, IN. She later moved to Indianapolis and obtained a juris doctorate from Indiana University School of Law, where she discovered an aptitude for writing, earning herself a spot on her school's Law Review. After practicing law for five years, Jai discovered her artistic talent through using her creative skills to litigate countless jury and bench trials. This inspired her to pursue her passion by harnessing her imagination to make fictional characters come to life.

Connect with Jai:
www.jaianddonisha.com
www.facebook.com/jaianddonisha
www.twitter.com/jaibunni
www.instagram.com/jai_darlene